THE
BOOK
without
WORDS

A Fable of
Medieval Magic

AVI

HYPERION BOOKS
FOR CHILDREN
NEW YORK

For Susan Raab

First Edition
1 3 5 7 9 10 8 6 4 2
Printed in the United States of America
This book is set in 14-point Celestia Antiqua.
Designed by Christine Kettner

Reinforced binding

Library of Congress Cataloging-in-Publication Data on file.
ISBN 0-7868-0829-2

Visit www.hyperionbooksforchildren.com

A *life unlived*
is like
a book without words

Old proverb

1

I T WAS IN the year 1046, on a cold winter's night, when a fog, thick as wool and dank as a dead man's hand, crept up from the River Scrogg into the ancient town of Fulworth. The fog settled like an icy shroud over the town, filling the mud-clogged streets and crooked lanes from Westgate to Bishopsgate, from Three Rats Quay upon the decaying riverbanks to Saint Osyth's Cathedral by the city center. It clung to the crumbling city walls. It heightened the stench of rotten hay and offal, of vinegary wine and rancid ale. It muffled the sound of pealing church bells calling the weary faithful to apprehensive prayers.

In a neglected corner of town, at the bottom of Clutterbuck Lane, with its grimy courtyard and noxious well, against the town's walls, stood a dilapidated two-story stone house. The first-level windows were blocked up with stone. A single second-floor window was curtained.

In a large room on the second floor stood a very old man by the name of Thorston. His dirty, high-cheek-boned face—with baggy eyes and long narrow nose—was deeply lined. His mouth was toothless. His eyes were green. Unkempt hair, hoary eyebrows, and wispy beard were as sparse as they were gray. He was wearing an old, torn blue robe to which was attached—at his waist—a small leather purse.

In the trembling light provided by an all but gut-tered candle, Thorston fed bits of sea coal into a brazier and watched its blaze change from red to blue. He sprinkled in some copper grains: the flames turned green.

"Green," whispered Thorston. "The color of life." The thought brought an anxious recollection of Brother Wilfrid's eyes. "No," he murmured. "There shall be no death for me."

He peered back into the room's shifting shadows. Nearest to him was a tar-black raven. The sleeping bird—his name was Odo—was perched on a cracked human skull that rested atop a column of leather-bound books.

Farther on, in a small back room, Thorston could see his servant girl, Sybil, asleep on her straw pallet. She had been with him for just four months and knew nothing about him—not who he was, not what he was doing—nothing.

The old man shuffled to his dirty, rumpled bed where the Book Without Words lay open. He read it. "Yes," he muttered, "one by one—in the proper sequence, at the proper moment, and I at the proper age."

He went back to the brazier. With twisted, twig-thin, and stained fingers, Thorston took up an iron pot and placed it over the green flames. "All is ready," he said.

With his left hand, he reached into a round box and removed a perfect cube of white clay. With his right hand, he kneaded the clay until it became as soft as the nape of a newborn's neck. With his left hand, he placed the clay at the bottom of the pot—in its exact center.

Weak heart fluttering with excitement, Thorston used his right hand to pour a flagon of water over the clay. The water was holy water siphoned secretly from the cathedral's baptismal font, then tinted pink with a drop of his own blood.

Taking the items from his hip purse, the old man rapidly added to the mix; bits of shredded gargoyle ears, chimera crumbs, scales from a fire-lizard's tail, two dozen white spider legs, thirteen and a half nightshade leaves, sixteen hairs from the tip of a Manx cat's tail, plus six white pearls of dried unicorn tears. He also dropped in the blackest of the raven's black feathers.

Using a spoon made of Jerusalem silver, Thorston

stirred the mixture eighty-six times to the left—once for each year of his life. He stirred to the right eighty-one more times—once for each day of his eighty-sixth year. When the brew smelled like the sweet breath of a resurrected phoenix, he knew he was close. His pulse quickened.

From the small leather purse on his belt, he drew forth a box made of narwhale bone. Within lay the dusty remains of Pythagoras, most ancient of philosophers. Thorston paused: the dust had cost him much—all the gold he could make—gold that would soon crumble. The other ingredients in the formula had taken more false gold. Thorston didn't care that it was false. His new life would make him—for all practical purposes—invisible. As he had planned things, by the time his gold turned to sand, he would not be found.

Thorston sprinkled Pythagoras's remains grain by grain into the pot, until the brew frothed, foamed, and fumed.

His excitement rising, Thorston scurried to his bed, checked the book anew, then hastened back to stir the recipe: one stir to the right—for the midnight sky. Three stirs to the left—for the heavenly Three. One stir across—for the noonday sun. A final stir for the cold and distant moon.

"Now," he said, unable to suppress his exhilaration, "the final ingredient . . . the girl's life."

In quite another part of Fulworth, a monk appeared at the entrance of a small and bleak cemetery. His name was Brother Wilfrid, and he too was very old. Indeed, his face was a web of wrinkles upon skin so thin, so translucent, the skull beneath offered up its own yellow cast. Upon his mottled head hung shreds of lank white hair. His small, green-hued eyes were sunk deep and forever leaking tears. His nose was all but fleshless, his mouth almost without lips. Knobby feet were bare. Stooped and limping, Brother Wilfrid wore an old brown tunic, more tattered than complete.

In one clawlike hand, he held up a smoldering torch. The light of the feeble flame seeped through the shifting veils of fog, a fog that drifted back and forth like the ebb and flow of open sea. The monk prowled about the cemetery, over the oozing black mire, pausing before cracked gravestones, holding his torch close to examine obscure names. From time to time he rubbed encrusted dirt away to read Latin or Runic words.

"Not here," he murmured at last.

Leaving his spent torch behind, the old monk limped out of the cemetery and into the church. It was a small, ancient structure built with gray stone. Its modest single tower was sharply pointed. Wilfrid entered by a narrow, arched doorway, stepping noiselessly into the building. It was deserted. On the old stone altar, a solitary candle burned, its muted light making the outer reaches of the building indistinct. But on the eastern wall was a large painting. Wilfrid looked at it and gasped. "Saint Elfleda!" he cried. The saint was portrayed larger than life, garbed in white, floating in the air. One hand held a belt, the other hand was lifted in blessing. Her large, dark eyes were almond-shaped and full of pain.

Wilfrid sank to his knees. "Help me," he pleaded. "Help me help you."

A short time later, the old monk left the church, went out into the roiling fog, and roamed through Fulworth, making his way along stinking, narrow streets, constricted lanes, and neglected courtyards. But in truth, Wilfrid did not look where he was going so much as he *sniffed*.

Suddenly he halted, lifted his frail head, and breathed deeply. He had smelled something. *Goat reek! Thorston's stink!* A smell he could never forget.

The monk, breathing deeply, old heart pounding, went on. His nose led him to a neglected corner of town, to the bottom of Clutterbuck Lane and its grimy courtyard centered by a fetid well. There, against the city's crumbling walls, he saw a dilapidated two-story stone house. But though the house appeared to contain no life, Brother Wilfrid stared at it, sniffed at it.

"Blessed Saint Elfleda," he whispered. "I've found him! Thorston *is* here." He sniffed again. This time he smelled gargoyle, chimera, fire-lizard, and . . . a raven. "God's mercy!" cried Wilfrid. "He's about to make the stones of life!"

The old monk stretched out a frail, trembling hand toward the house. "Return the book to me!" he called in a rasping voice.

No reply. Wilfrid hardly expected one. Worse, as he stood there, he knew he was too feeble to take back the book himself. He would need help. But who would help him? He sniffed again. This time he detected—a girl. A *young* girl.

Of course! If Thorston were working to renew his life by making the stones, he would need some young person's breath—and then *her* life.

He must talk to her and warn her before it was too late.

3

Thorston crept into the back room, where Sybil, covered by a thin, moth-eaten wool blanket, lay asleep on a straw pallet. Thorston gazed at her. She was big boned, and skinny. Long brown hair was tangled; face chapped and sullied; her nose—often dripping—was blunt and red from the chill. She had on a tattered, gray wool gown with wide sleeves, which she wore night and day. Most important of all—for Thorston—was the fact that she was as young as he had been when he stole the book: thirteen years of age. Now her breath would become *his* breath—his life. When he regained his young life, she would die. What does her life matter? thought Thorston. She's nobody. No one will miss or care about her. It's *my* life I desire.

He bent over the girl. With a quick, scooping gesture, he caught up a fistful of her sleepy breath—a hand bowl, as it were, of her life. He clapped his other hand over it, trapping it.

Back at the brazier, the old man let Sybil's breath slide through his thin fingers into the pot. The brew seethed, frothed, and boiled, then settled into a slow simmer.

Though Thorston's heart pounded so hard he experienced some dizziness, he plunged his right hand into the hot concoction. Paying no heed to the searing pain, he pressed down to the pot's bottom. There—in the midst of thick and sticky sludge—he found *four stones*.

Breathless with excitement, knowing he must hurry, Thorston plucked up the largest stone. It was white, round, and an inch in diameter. He clutched it in his trembling hand. With faltering steps, he staggered to the window at the front of the house, where he drew aside the leather curtain that kept in and out the light.

Outside, the thick fog had made the night sky impenetrable. But as Thorston stood before the window, clenched fist lifted heavenward, the mists parted. A full moon blossomed. From it, a glittering shaft of gold light fell like an arrow upon his quaking hand.

Thorston counted to thirteen—slowly—before drawing down his hand. Though it was growing difficult, even painful for him to breathe, he unfolded his fingers and peered into his palm.

There lay the piece he had taken from the pot. It had turned *green*.

"I have it," he whispered with breathless ferocity. "Life! Three more stones, and I shall be reborn."

But even as Thorston exalted, a sharp pain squeezed his heart. His left arm turned numb. His right eye fogged. As he struggled for breath, it became hard for him to grip the stone. "Spirits of mortality," he gasped. "What's amiss?"

His heart gave a jolt.

Thorston lurched across the room. Tripping on a pot, he started to fall. In a panic, he stuffed the green stone into his gaping, toothless mouth, and with a desperate gulp, swallowed it. Even so, he collapsed onto his bed. "Save me!" he shrieked. "Save the stones of life!"

There lay Thorston—all but dead.

4

Thorston's cry woke Odo the raven. The bird lifted his head and looked about the dismal room. When he saw his master sprawled on the bed, he flapped his wings and squawked, "Wings of salvation. What is wrong?"

A flutter of wings, some jumps and a hop—Odo could not fly—brought the raven to the old man's chest. "Master," he said, peering into Thorston's wizened face. "It's me, Odo, your most loving, your most faithful of servants. What ails you?"

"I've begun," muttered the old man, "my rebirth. But . . . I may be too . . . *old*."

Odo cocked his head. "*Gold*, Master? Did you say you made *gold*?"

"Yes . . . old . . . and dying."

"*Dying*, dear Master? But did you make gold?"

"Just . . . the first . . . step," the old man whispered, "toward new life. If I'm to live, I must reveal the secret."

"*Me*, Master," cried the raven. "Reveal the gold-making secret to *me*!"

"No. The . . . girl."

"*Sybil?*"

"Yes, her."

"Kind master," croaked the bird. "Gentle master! I'm sure you didn't mean to say that. You know she's a fool. A street beggar. A nothing. Don't you remember? You promised that when you finally made gold, it would be me that would get half."

"Fetch . . . the girl," Thorston whispered, even as his eyes clouded and his toothless jaw went slack.

5

Odo stared at the old man in disbelief. He pecked on his bony chest. "Most generous of masters, speak to me!"

When Thorston did not respond, Odo looked about the room. Spying the boiling pot, he leaped from the bed, clawed his way to the brazier, and stood upon the pot's hot rim. Hopping about its edge, he peered inside. The rising vapors caused his eyes to tear. He could see nothing.

Livid, talons hurting, Odo leaped away and began

a frantic search about the cluttered room. He skipped under the bed, around it, on it. Nothing. He climbed on the table. Nothing. Crawled under it. Nothing. Coming upon an upside-down copper pot, he attempted to poke his beak under its rim in case anything was hidden beneath. When it proved too heavy, he darted a glance back toward the rear room to make certain Sybil was asleep. She was. He checked Thorston: the old man's eyes remained shut.

Satisfied he was unobserved, the raven lifted his left claw, held it toward the pot, and hissed: "*Risan— Risan.*" The pot rose into the air where it hovered unsteadily. Odo looked beneath. Nothing. The next moment the pot fell with a crash.

Furious, the raven hopped back to the old man and pried back each of his fingers. *Nothing.* He jumped to Thorston's chest and drew close to his face. "Master!" he screamed, black tongue sticking out. "Think how loyally I've served you. In your solitary days, I alone talked to you. When you were hungry, I fetched food for you. When you were sick, I watched over you. Brought herbs to you. Guarded you from the world. Kept watch for dangers. To prove my loyalty, I gave up flying, my bird essence, allowing myself to become almost human—for you. Be grateful, Master. Be open handed. Tell me how to make gold. I want to fly again!"

The old man remained mute.

"Birds of mercy," hissed Odo. "He's truly dying. Cruel Master!" he suddenly shrieked. "Liar! Cheat! Self-centered knave! Hateful human! You're betraying me. What's to be done?" With a violent shake of his head, the bird peered down the hallway toward the back room. The thought that he would have to share his master's gold-making secret with the new servant girl filled him with fury. But with Thorston dying, there was no choice. Swallowing his rage, Odo leaped off the bed and hopped down the hallway. Upon reaching the girl, he leaned forward and gave a sharp peck to her hand. "Sybil! Wake!" he croaked. "Master Thorston is dying. Get up!"

The girl woke slowly. "Wh—at?" she murmured.

"Master is calling you."

"Is it to cook, fetch . . . or run an errand?" Sybil said as she rolled away from the bird and pressed down into the thin straw. "Is he too lazy to look for something himself?"

"Sybil, he's *dying*."

"Who's dying?

"Master."

The girl rubbed her eyes. "Is he—really?"

"Yes, and he wants to tell you the secret of making gold."

"You're jesting."

Odo, his panic growing, shook his head. "Sybil, know the truth: Master is an . . . alchemist."

For a moment Sybil remained on her back, staring upward. Then she said, "I don't know the word."

"An *alchemist* is someone who makes *gold*."

"Are you saying that Master Thorston . . . makes . . . gold?"

"Yes."

"Then I'm England's queen."

"Idiot, what do you think he's been trying to do these past few months?"

"How would I know? He barely speaks to me."

The bird leaped atop the girl's head and gave her nose a rap with his beak. "Stupid girl—if he reveals the secret, we can live like lords."

Sybil wiped her nose with the back of her hand. "Odo, four months ago he took me in from the streets. I'm his servant. Nothing more."

"Sit up!"

When Sybil pushed herself up, the bird dropped to her knees and peered up into her face. She stared back at him. Odo was almost two feet long, from black, curved beak, to hunched back, to stiff tail. Though his

14

black feathers were without sheen, his eyes were as bright as polished ebony. His talons were sharp.

"Sybil," he croaked, "you're an orphan. You're attached to no one. Not to me. Not to anyone. Do you think—when he dies—that anyone will give you food and shelter?"

Sybil considered the raven's words. When Master had taken her up, she was grateful. Oddly, all he had cared about was her age. As for his house, it mattered nothing to her that it was filthy and chaotic. Nor did she mind the work, any more than she considered Thorston's silent, reclusive life. Winter was approaching. She had a roof above. Something to eat. It was enough.

As for Odo—at first she had found it odd that he talked. But from the moment she had arrived the bird had belittled her, bossed her about. Though self-effacing to Master, he never said a kind word to her—he was ever snide or cynical. But wasn't that the way people always talked to her? It might as well be so with a bird. Though she didn't trust him, she had to admit he was right: if Master died, she'd have even less than she had now.

She looked about. In the dim light she could see the little room that was her domain: cold and dirty stone walls. No windows. A straw pallet. A few rusty iron pots and cracked wooden spoons. Some chipped clay pots that contained food: dry, salted fish; cabbage; turnip bits; and barley grains. A damp, dreary chill that made her shiver. She supposed Odo was correct: it could get worse.

"Odo," she said, "please, is Master *truly* dying?"

"Do not all men die? And when he does," said the raven, "I suppose even brainless girls like you might appreciate some gold."

"You're mocking me."

"Sybil, listen!" cried the bird. "He has made gold. I'm sure of it. If we don't find it, or learn how he makes it, we'll have to steal to stay alive. Get caught stealing, and Master Bashcroft, the city reeve, will put us in jail and hang us."

"I haven't told you," said Sybil, "but Master has been sending me to the apothecary quite often."

"Of course he did! He was working on the gold-making secret."

"When I bought those things Master wanted— gargoyle ears, spider legs—the apothecary began asking questions about him."

"Mistress Weebly is a meddlesome fool."

"But the last time I went, Master Bashcroft watched me from the street."

"You should have told me," said the bird. "The moment that vast man learns of Master Thorston's death and discovers there's no heir, he'll seize the house. He won't care dead slugs about a stupid servant girl and a raven that can't fly. He'll throw us onto the streets. In less than two weeks *we'll* be dead, dumped into shallow paupers' graves, and left to rot and stink. I suppose even you can hope for something more than death."

Sybil rubbed her eyes, her nose. "All right," she said after a few moments. "I'll go to him."

7

Sybil padded down the dim hallway into the large front room. The wooden floor, worn and uneven, was icy to her bare feet. Odo came right behind, his claws *tip-tap*ping as he hopped along.

Candlelight revealed the clutter: Thorston's apparatus—pestles, bone cups, mortars, vials, kuttrolf bottles, flagons, and funnels—lay strewn about. Tilted and broken shelves were laden with glass jars, wooden boxes, and clay vessels. Books, screeds, and parchment had been cast about at random. A cracked human skull, capped by a wig of bird droppings, sat atop a pile of moldy books. The brazier contained a small green flame, which crackled and popped. Aside from the iron pot whose boiling contents spewed thick, foul fumes, everything was encrusted with dust, filth, and cobwebs.

In the four months Sybil had been there, the room had not been cleaned. She wondered if it ever had been. But she was never allowed to touch anything until a crisis erupted. Then, though Master worked at night when she slept, he'd roar: "Where's the pestle?" or some such. All was in tumult until she found what he'd misplaced, usually right under his sharp nose.

As for money, as far as Sybil knew, Master never seemed to have much. When she went marketing he rarely gave her more than a farthing or a groat. Only at the apothecary did he pay more.

"Tell me what happened," said Sybil.

"He seems to have collapsed." The bird indicated the brazier with his beak. "I think he was working there."

Sybil looked at the brazier just in time to see the fire die, the coals turn to ash, and the muck in the pot cease to bubble. The stench remained.

"God's breath," she muttered as she looked about. "What a gross reek." She peered through the gloom and saw Thorston on his disheveled bed. Feeble and dried up, his long, big-knuckled hands lay by his sides, twitching spasmodically.

Though the stink in the room made her want to gag, she forced herself close. "Master," she called. "It's me. Sybil. Did you call?"

His jaws working as if chewing a tiny object, Thorston partly opened his eyes. He beckoned with a crooked finger. "Girl," he whispered, "if I'm . . . to live, I must reveal . . . the secret of the book."

"He's talking about that book," whispered Sybil. "Odo, I may be ignorant, but even I know you have to be mad to read a book that has no words."

"Never mind the book," Odo whispered into her ear. "Ask him about gold."

"Master," said Sybil, "tell me tell me how to make gold."

"No—it's the . . . stones of life which I . . . speak," the old man struggled to say. "They promise . . . life. Keep them . . . safe, so I may . . . continue to live."

"Master," said Sybil, "it's not stones that Odo and I need to live, but gold. Tell me how to make it."

"The secret is . . . here." Thorston's hands crawled over the Book Without Words like a crippled spider. "You must find someone with green eyes to read . . . the proper sequence."

"Master," said Sybil, "your book has no words."

"No, no, the magic of immortality . . . *is* . . . here. Don't let him . . . get it."

"H*im*?" asked Sybil. "Who are you talking about?"

"The green-eyed one . . ."

"Master, it's *you* who have green eyes."

Thorston's eyes widened with fright. "Keep him away!" he cried.

Even as he spoke, the twisted hand that lay upon the book fluttered like a broken moth, then lay perfectly still.

"God of mercy," Sybil whispered. "He's dead."

8

"Dead!" shrieked Odo. "Didn't I tell you to hurry?" Wings beating wildly, the raven leaped onto Thorston's chest, peered into his face, and pecked his lower lip. When there was no response the bird shook his head and crouched, muttering to himself.

Sybil trembled. She could hardly draw breath. All that Odo had warned her about—eviction, abandonment, starvation, and death—burst upon her like the clap of a cathedral bell. What would become of her!

She reached out and touched Thorston's wrist. To her surprise, she felt a feeble pulse. Next moment, she saw the old man's chest rise and fall. A surge of relief passed through her. "Odo!" she cried. "Master hasn't died. He lives!"

"It no longer matters," moaned Odo. "Dead or alive. He's addled and we're undone."

"Not if we find a green-eyed person," said the girl.

The bird whipped his head about. "What are you saying?"

"Only what Master said: his secrets are in his book, but they can be read by a green-eyed person."

"What he said was: we needed to keep the book *away* from green-eyed persons."

"Then you," said the girl, "are as vacant of brain as that skull upon which you sit. You said he was confused. He must have been talking about himself. Well, then, his secret is in the book. We need to find someone with green eyes to read it."

"Are you actually suggesting," said Odo, "we walk about this wretched city peering into people's *eyes*?"

"If we want those secrets, we will."

"Sybil, alchemy is *illegal*. It's considered sorcery. A hanging offense."

"But you said if we didn't learn how to make gold we'll perish," returned the girl. "Now, be still. I need to think how to find a green-eyed person."

"You *can't* think, so don't waste your time. You're nothing!" said the raven, and he retreated to his skull to sulk.

9

Sybil went to her favorite place—she could only go there when Thorston slept—the small, round, thick-glassed front window. She looked out. The weather with its dark, cold fog was, as always, nasty. How she longed for spring with its soft breezes, flowers, and warm sun.

Shifting slightly, Sybil caught sight of her likeness in the glass. Despising her looks; despising the fact that she was a worthless, ignorant, homely girl; despising how dependent she was, she turned away. Odo was right: she *was* alone in the world. A *nothing*. But Odo was right about another thing: knowing how to make gold would change her life.

She started: for a moment she thought she saw someone standing in the courtyard shadows, observing their house. A small person. A child, perhaps. She looked again. The figure was gone. I've become as addle-pated as Master, she thought.

Leaning on the window, she resumed her musings. If a green-eyed person was needed, how could she find one? Seeing the person in the courtyard gave her an idea.

"Odo," she said, "I think we should seek out a green-eyed *child*."

"A child? Why?"

"Children are easy to control. They won't ask questions."

"But few can read."

"It's only green eyes that are necessary."

"And how do you intend to find such?"

"I'll invent something to say to the merchants from whom I market."

"What of Master's rule that no one know of his existence?"

"Your eyes are black. Mine, brown. Our sole hope is to find a green-eyed person."

"Hope!" hissed Odo. "*Nothings* don't hope."

"I *won't* be nothing," cried Sybil. Eyes welling with tears, she ran into the back room and threw herself upon her straw pallet. If I'm to survive, she thought as she smeared away the wetness on her cheeks, I need to find a green-eyed child. With that, she began to compose the speech she would give to merchants on the morrow. She would start with the apothecary, Mistress Weebly. She was closest.

10

Odo, on his skull, stared at the pot that sat upon the brazier. He was convinced gold was in it, gold that Thorston had made. Not that Odo had any intention of sharing it with Sybil. Not a grain. But, he told himself, to get it will take patience—and cunning.

11

In another part of town, Ambrose Bashcroft, the city

reeve of Fulworth—the man in charge of the city's law and order—lay in his quilted bed propped up by a dozen goose-down pillows. The bed, curtained round with heavy wool, provided him with an effective cocoon of self-importance.

A big man, Bashcroft was broad as a barrel and not much taller, his bulky body much given to jigs and jounces. His head was rooted upon a short, wide neck, and was beetle browed with bristling eyebrows, one slightly lower than the other. With pendulant jowls and enough chins to serve as palace steps, Bashcroft looked more bullish than most bulls.

"*Dura lex, sed lex*" was the sole Latin legal phrase Bashcroft knew, but, liking its meaning—*The law is hard, but it is the law*—he used it as both the anvil and hammer of his office. For to this phrase he always added, "And since I am the law, it therefore follows, I must be hard."

As far as the reeve was concerned, it was his duty, his obligation, to keep Fulworth beneath his outsized thumb. And in the exercise of this power, his silent partner was Mistress Weebly.

Mistress Weebly was the town apothecary, a profession that enabled her to gather information about town inhabitants. Not only did she provide physic for the sick and dying, she offered potions, tonics, and charms to those suffering from other kinds of afflictions, real or imagined. That's to say, broken arms or broken hearts were all one to Mistress Weebly. A woman of insatiable curiosity, she traded in rumor, gossip, and scandal the way a merchant trades in goods. And *everything* she gleaned by way of personal information was of the greatest interest to the reeve.

Their arrangement was this: she told him what she learned; he protected her from the occasional questions raised about the advice she offered and the odd things she sold.

So it was that Mistress Weebly had informed Bashcroft about the girl who had recently come to town, the one who appeared in her shop with a raven on her shoulder. And when this girl began to buy such things as spider's legs, white clay, and fire-lizard's tail, the reeve and Mistress Weebly were even more interested. But other than the girl's name—Sybil—they knew very little.

Bashcroft had ordered Mistress Weebly to learn more about the girl. For whom did she work? Where did she live? And, most of all, what was the purpose of such odd purchases?

As the reeve shifted his corpulent bulk to find a tad of comfort on his bed, he made up his mind he would speak to the apothecary on the morrow.

CHAPTER TWO

1

THE EARLY morning was cold and damp when a shivering Sybil stepped from Thorston's house into the muddy, ice-encrusted courtyard. Odo, hunched on her shoulder, gripped her shawl so tightly his talons pricked her skin.

"Sybil," he croaked into her ear as the girl walked toward the city center, "must I say it again: Master insisted no one must learn of his existence, much less enter the house."

"Master is all but dead," said Sybil. "If we're to get the gold-making secret we have to do *something*."

"But you said the apothecary has been asking questions," said the bird. "And what of the reeve? You claimed he was watching you. You may be a fool, but those people aren't."

"I'm not a fool," Sybil protested.

Odo shook his head in dismay. "A fool is the first to think himself wise but last to know it isn't so. Oh, I do wish I could fly away."

"Where would you go?"

"Master once told me about a land called Italy. He said the sky was always blue and warm. Flowers are beautiful. Bright colors are on walls. People sing while they work. Even the drying laundry looks like flags of celebration."

"Could I go with you?"

"Can worms sing?"

Stung, Sybil said, "You think only of yourself."

"I don't like to waste my—"

"Shhh!" Sybil whispered. "People are ahead. It will prove a disaster if you're heard talking."

They made their silent way through the narrow, crowded streets of Fulworth, passing merchants with sickly faces, empty hands, and even emptier purses; passing porters and traders hauling meager goods on backs or in broken barrows; passing an old ox pulling a cart of steaming dung, making his laborious, slipping, sliding way. Black-robed priests and nuns crept along the high street, clutching rosary beads and wooden crosses in chilled hands as cold lips whispered pensive prayers; goodwives, few with parcels, hastened past street-level shops, whose lowered shutters offered more icicles than goods. Troves of foot-stamping, teeth-chattering paupers were already begging and were already being ignored. And among the throng was Brother Wilfrid.

As Sybil and Odo went by, the old monk, catching a whiff of Thorston's goat reek, whirled about. He spotted Odo first, then Sybil. *His stink is on that raven,* he reasoned. *That must be the girl I detected. The one I need to help me. The one in peril.*

He began to follow.

Sybil, unaware she was being pursued, reached the apothecary, a small shop wedged between a potter's store and a scrivener. She paused beneath its painted symbol, a unicorn horn, to recall the speech she had prepared.

"Sybil . . ." whispered the bird in warning.

"Shhh," said the girl as she opened the door and stepped inside.

2

The apothecary's shop was a small, crowded room walled with shelves that bore bottles and jars containing roots, like ginger; herbs, like mandragora; spices, like cloves; powdered minerals, like lead; ointments like spikenard.

Opposite the doorway was a low trestle table upon which had been placed a mortar and pestle plus a copper balance scale. An oil lamp provided meager light. A little mirror hung on one wall. Behind the table stood Mistress Weebly, the apothecary.

Everything about Mistress Weebly was small: small body; small face; small, gimlet eyes; small nose. Her smallness was emphasized by her being dressed in an overlarge, soiled gown of green that reached her ankles—sleeves pinched at her wrists, apron over all, wimple on her head. It was as if she had been dropped into a dirty sack and was spying out from it. Indeed, the woman's only largeness was her curiosity.

Standing next to her was Damian Perbeck, her apprentice. He was plucking rosemary leaves from stems and chopping them into tiny pieces with a small knife. The boy was fourteen years old. He was somewhat plump; his fair hair had been clipped round his head like an inverted bowl. His red, splotchy face bore sleepy eyes, turned-up nose, and turned-down lips, all of which he marshaled to provide a mask of indifference.

"Good morrow, Mistress Weebly," said Sybil, closing the door and cutting a curtsy. She noticed the boy, but she made no greeting.

"Ah, Maid Sybil," returned the little woman, her

voice squeaky and shrill. "How fare you this cold morning?"

"Chilly, Mistress," said Sybil, her eyes cast down as befit her station.

"And how," said the woman, "does your master's health bode this morning?" She brought her small hands together as if in prayer.

"Mistress Weebly," began Sybil in a low voice as she embarked upon the speech she had prepared, "I fear my master is gravely ill. And—"

"God grant him a speedy recovery," interrupted the apothecary.

She turned to Damian. "You, now," she said, abruptly boxing him on the ear. "Get away from here. Continue your work in the back room. Go!" She all but pushed the boy out the door at the back of the shop. Only then did she turn back to Sybil.

"Now, then, my dear maid, I should like to pray for your master's good health. But it's difficult to do so without knowing his name. Would you be kind enough to share it with me?"

Sybil, taken by surprise, stammered, "It's . . . Master Thorston. But—"

"I've never heard of him, I fear. Has he been in town long?"

"I don't know. But—"

"These things you purchase for him, Maid Sybil,

they're most unusual. Just between us what *does* he do with them?"

Odo moved uneasily on Sybil's shoulder, his talons digging into her.

"I know nothing of such matters, Mistress Weebly," returned Sybil in haste. "I'm but Master's house drudge, there to moil his filth and cook his swill."

"Are you his only servant?"

"I am, Mistress."

"And is your Master Thorston young or old?"

Sybil, feeling she was losing control of the conversation, whispered, "Very old."

"Alas," said the apothecary, "advanced age and illness oft step the dance of death. Is he near his end?"

"Oh . . . no . . . I assure you—"

"But you did say he was sick. Perhaps I can provide useful physic."

Sybil hardly knew what to say.

"Maid Sybil," pressed the apothecary, "I must say this: within my little head lingers a lengthy list of your master's requests: fire-lizard's tail, hairs from a Manx cat's tail, unicorn tears—among other such oddments. Pray now," said the little woman, leaning forward in conspiratorial fashion, "could he be dabbling in the alchemic arts—making *gold*?"

"Please, Mistress," whispered Sybil in great alarm, "I assure you, I know nothing of such things."

31

Mistress Weebly, enjoying Sybil's discomfort, smiled. "But if your master *should* die," she said, "hasten here. I'll provide real coin for those secrets of his you've managed to glean."

"Mistress Weebly," said Sybil, "I promise you, I know of no such secrets. But if you please," she said, desperate to speak what she had planned to say, "only yesterday a child came to our door and—"

"And where pray, *is* that door?"

"Clutterbuck Lane," Sybil blurted out and raced on: "The child was asking for my master. I had to send it away, for as I told you, Master Thorston is ill. Alas, the child went so quickly I neglected to ask a name. But I did notice green eyes. Know you, Mistress, of any such child in town? One with . . . green eyes?"

The apothecary's small eyes narrowed: "Boy or girl?" she asked.

"In faith, Mistress, I know not. The child was bundled so against the chill."

"But," the woman said, "all the same—you noticed *green* eyes?"

Sybil, feeling panicky, nodded and moved toward the door, only to pause: "Pray, Mistress Weebly; please send any such green-eyed child you know to my master's house. He'd be much obliged."

"To Master Thorston of Clutterbuck Lane," said the apothecary, "a green-eyed child. I shall surely try."

Sybil stepped out upon the street as quickly as she could.

"You are a fool," rasped Odo the moment they left the shop. "You gave everything away."

"I didn't expect so many questions," Sybil admitted.

"You even told her about his alchemy."

"Odo," gasped Sybil. "The reeve is approaching."

Master Bashcroft was marching down the narrow street toward them. Two steel-helmeted soldiers, pointed pikes in hand, trailed behind.

Sybil, eyes averted, hastily stepped aside and dropped a curtsy as the reeve passed by. Bashcroft did not so much as glance at her.

"By Saint Modoc," the girl whispered as soon as he had passed, "I swear that man has been spying on me."

"Then take us home," snapped Odo. "Where it's safe. And no more talk of green-eyed children."

"What about master's gold-making secret?" said Sybil.

"All we can do is pray he regains his speech," said the bird.

"I doubt he will," muttered a disappointed Sybil. She set off, paying no attention to Brother Wilfrid, who was observing her closely as she hurried through the muddy streets back toward Clutterbuck Lane.

3

Should I follow? the monk wondered. No. She's with that raven—who talks. Such magic is surely Thorston's work. Which means the bird is his underling. I'll have to speak to the girl alone.

Wilfrid observed the reeve watching the girl. Why is he so concerned with her? he asked himself. I'd best keep my eye on him as well.

4

Bashcroft watched Sybil and Odo until the two turned a corner and were lost to his view. Telling the soldiers to wait, he shoved open the door to the apothecary shop and stomped inside.

"Master Bashcroft," cried Mistress Weebly when the large man banged his staff down on the floor with a loud crack of authority. "God grant us days of greater warmth."

"That maid—" said Bashcroft, giving no pause

for civility, "the one with a raven on her shoulder. She was just here. What have you learned?"

The apothecary's small hands went together so quickly it was hard to know if she were praying or applauding. Smiling, she said, "She is servant to one Master Thorston."

"I never heard of the man."

"He resides at the end of Clutterbuck Lane."

"But no one could live there without my knowledge," exclaimed Bashcroft, who, being a man who thought he knew everything, cast doubt on all he didn't know.

"Apparently he does."

"What else?" said Bashcroft.

"I've compiled a list of all the things the girl has purchased for this Master Thorston. It's the kind of things one would want for"—she leaned forward—"alchemy."

"*Alchemy!*" roared the reeve, giving way to a rare moment of honest astonishment. "Has he truly made gold?"

"I don't know."

"What more did you learn?"

"He seems to be ill," said Mistress Weebly. "Indeed, Master Reeve, as I read signs, I believe this Thorston fellow is *dying*."

"Dying!"

Mistress Weebly smiled. "But even as he dies, he's in need of—a green-eyed child."

"For what purpose?"

"I believe," said the apothecary, "for his alchemy."

"Mistress Weebly," proclaimed the reeve, drawing himself up to the full bulk of his bluster, "alchemy, being unnatural, is an offense against all nature, its practice treason against the state. Moreover, all those who gain by such acts are equally guilty—with dire punishments for those engaged. Confiscation of property will occur. Removal of a finger may be necessary. A hand, perhaps. Even a head. Depending. Depending on me. *Dura lex, sed lex.* I am the law, and I am hard."

"And," simpered the apothecary, "how glad I am that such power rests with you."

"Mistress Weebly," said Bashcroft. "In exercise of that power, I hereby put you under house arrest."

"Arrest!" cried the apothecary.

"This information about Master Thorston's alchemy," said the reeve, "is much too dangerous to be allowed to flow freely among the ignorant public. Rumors of it will cause excitement. Excitement will cause expectations to rise. Large expectations in small minds are a menace that must be always suppressed, else riots will follow. For, beyond all else, it's my duty to protect the citizens of Fulworth."

"But, Master Reeve, you and I have been partners and—"

"Silence! When I resolve this matter you'll be free.

For now, do not leave these premises. Speak to no one about this. Not even to your apprentice. I shall post a soldier by the door."

Without further ado, the reeve stormed out of the shop.

5

After arranging for a guard to remain at the apothecary's door, Bashcroft mulled over what he had learned: a Master Thorston, residing in town but hiding, was a dying man practicing alchemy. Making *gold*.

Bashcroft could only feel that the secret of how to make gold would be an extraordinary stroke of luck and fortune—in his own hands. He considered his position: he had insufficient wealth. Without wealth, there is no real authority. Without real authority, there is no dignity. Without dignity, chaos comes. If chaos reigns, the world is undone. Undo the world, and you strike against God's very creation. Therefore, for him, Ambrose Bashcroft, to live in poverty was a sin against God Himself.

If this Master Thorston was in need of a child with green eyes, then he—Bashcroft—would place just such a child in that household—and gather the gold-making secret for himself. But it must be done in haste—before the old man expired. Happily, Bashcroft knew where to secure such a child. So resolved, he headed for the banks of the River Scrogg—the poorest part of Fulworth.

6

Mistress Weebly was furious. She cursed herself for being such a dupe. Why had she so trusted the reeve that she gave him all that information about Master Thorston? It was perfectly clear to her that Bashcroft was going to take advantage of her information for his profit. But she—more than anyone—could make use of it. Did *she* not have all the ingredients required to make gold? All that was wanting was the formula.

Greatly agitated, she pushed open the rear door, shoving Damian away, who had been standing on the other side.

"Were you listening?" she demanded.

"Of course not, Mistress," said the boy as meekly as he knew how.

"See that you don't," she said, boxing his ear for good measure. "Now, go and attend the shop. My head hurts. I must lie down." She went directly off to bed.

Damian, his ear smarting, came into the shop. But

it wasn't only the blow that was causing his ear to tingle: he *had* been listening, and heard all about Master Thorston and his alchemy.

He went right to the little mirror and studied his eyes. Not completely green, he thought. They contain flecks of blue. Still, close enough. "Indeed, I'm tired of being an apprentice," he muttered. "I'm fit for better things."

So it was that Damian made up his mind: the next morning he would go to this house on Clutterbuck Lane. This Master Thorston was apparently old, sick, and dying. Easy enough to pry the gold-making secret from him. As for this Sybil—she being the only servant, and a maid, he had no doubt he could dominate her.

Moreover, Damian vowed that once he had gold coins and knew how to make more, he'd run away from this obnoxious apprenticeship and live the life of a wealthy freeman.

7

Ambrose Bashcroft, in search of a green-eyed boy, made his loud and lumbering way through narrow, muddy alleys and back ways, until he reached the banks of the River Scrogg. There, amid moldering wharves, paltry chandler shops, and dilapidated hovels, were to be found the homeless men, women, and children of Fulworth, those who eked out their empty lives in desolation.

Whenever the reeve came upon an assemblage of such folk, he approached them, banged his staff upon the ground to draw their attention, and cried out: "Pay heed! Pay heed! I, Ambrose Bashcroft, the city reeve of Fulworth, am offering you the privilege of helping me. Hear me well: I am in lawful need of a green-eyed child. I shall pay two pennies for such a child. All who have one to offer may approach me humbly now."

When no one came, he scowled and moved on.

So did Brother Wilfrid, who had heard it all.

8

The old monk meandered though the city's poor quarter. In his ragged robe and with his emaciated appearance, he looked so like a local inhabitant that they paid him scant attention.

He had considered any number of children before he found one sleeping against a building. He was a wretchedly thin and dirty boy with an ill-fitting smock and hole-ridden boots. But what attracted Wilfrid to him was the tangle of dark red hair that fell off his face. And when Wilfrid looked down upon him, and the boy, who had been asleep, started and looked up, he did so with—green eyes.

"Please, sir," said the boy, scrambling to his feet, "is something the matter?"

"What are you doing here?" asked Wilfrid.

"I live about, sir," said the boy, staring at Wilfrid's ancient face with the repugnance youth reserves for age.

"No home?"

"No, sir."

"No family?"

"Dead, sir."

"What is your name?"

"Alfric, sir."

"When have you last eaten?"

"Three days ago."

"Would you like some bread?"

"Yes, please."

"Listen to me," said the monk, "I am in search of a book without words. Help me recover it, and you will earn some bread."

"A book, sir? With no words?"

"'Tis so. Now, come with me," said Wilfrid.

Alfric was hesitant but hungry. And hunger, having least, often risks most. He chose to follow the monk.

9

Night came to Fulworth. In the upper room at the house at the end of Clutterbuck Lane, a solitary rush candle provided a glimmer of languishing light. Upon the bed lay Master Thorston, eyes closed. Near to his hand was the Book Without Words; Odo insisted it stay there in case Master recovered his senses. But though the small rise and fall of his chest suggested life, he had not uttered a word since the day before.

Sybil, sure her master would not speak, sat on a three-legged stool next to his bed. The room was chilly enough to see her vaporous breath in the gloom. A chipped clay bowl filled with warm bone broth rested in her lap. Though the broth was for her master, she welcomed its heat. Now and again she tried to feed him.

No one spoke until low rumblings of thunder made her lift her head. "There will be a storm soon," she said, as much to herself as Odo.

Drawing her dirty shawl tighter around her shoulders, she studied Thorston's slack, withered face. What secrets, she wondered, lay within?

"Odo," she said after a while, "how long have you been with Master?"

"Too long."

"In all that time, did you ever learn any of his secrets?"

"The lengthier the life, the more locked the lip," said the bird.

Sybil rubbed her tired eyes. "That's not an answer to my question."

The raven shook his head. Sybil, knowing the bird was not about to tell her anything, sighed. Restless, deciding her efforts to feed Thorston were of no use, she put the bowl aside and went to the front window and gazed out. The courtyard was deserted. Or was it? There, where she had seen a figure the night before, she again thought she saw someone.

"Odo," she called.

"What?" said the raven, his voice sleepy. He had jumped to the skull.

Sybil peered into the courtyard again. Whoever she had seen had gone. She was disappointed.

"All this has exhausted me," murmured Odo. "I need my sleep. You keep watch on Master." He crouched on a stack of books.

Sybil made no reply. Doubting Master would ever wake, she wondered if it would not be better to leave right away. It was bad luck to be in a house when a man died. In any case, when Master died—which could not be long—her own life here would end. But where could she go? Other than servant's work, she didn't know what to do. As for the world beyond Fulworth, she knew nothing more than the wretched village where she had been raised, where her peasant parents had lived—if one could call it that—and died.

There was that *Italy* Odo had mentioned. It sounded wonderful. Sybil wondered if she could walk to it.

"Odo," she called. "How far off is that *Italy*?"

"Find it . . . yourself," murmured the bird, all but asleep.

No, thought Sybil, I can't even go there. Not till I have gold—which I'll never have. But I must do something.

She gazed out the window. The person had returned. As she considered him, it occurred to Sybil that he was rather childlike in size. And as she continued to gaze, she had the distinct sensation he was looking right at her. Perhaps, she suddenly thought, it's a green-eyed child!

She looked to Odo. The bird was sound asleep. Suddenly she felt pleased with herself. *Here's my chance to show him my plan was right!*

She crept down to the ground level, a large, empty area whose window spaces had been filled in with stone and mortar. The front door was kept closed by a heavy crossbeam. The rear wall—behind the central steps—was, in fact, part of the decaying city wall. An entryway had once existed there, but it too had been filled in with stone.

But there was nothing in the room save a pair of shovels used for disposing of night soil. In the room's center was a trapdoor that led to a dirt basement. Only Thorston—who had never gone out—had descended. Sybil preferred to use the outside privy.

She used both hands to lift the front-door crossbar. Noiselessly, she set it on the floor, then pulled open the door. Cold air blew in. Thunder rumbled again, closer. Trembling from the chill as well as nervousness, Sybil hesitated. She adjusted her shawl. Reminding herself she was only searching to see if a green-eyed child had come, she stepped out and set off across the courtyard. She had almost reached the well when a figure stepped from the shadows and blocked her way.

10

Sybil halted and gasped. Though the face was partly obscured by a monk's cowl, this wasn't a child, but a man.

"You come from that house," said Brother Wilfrid,

his voice weak and raspy. "Does a man called Thorston live there?"

"Y—es."

"Is he in possession of a book that has no words?"

Sybil, taken by surprise, said, "What can it matter to you?"

"Everything."

"What do you want?"

"Your help," said Wilfrid.

Even as he spoke a crack of lightning flooded the courtyard with white light. Simultaneously, a puff of wind blew back Wilfrid's hood. Sybil saw his face: it was as if she were looking at a living skull, some green-eyed *dead* thing that had, though hideous with decrepitude, somehow survived. Unnerved, she turned and fled.

"Stop!" the monk cried after her. "I need you. And you need me!"

11

Sybil ran back into the house, and replaced the crossbeam to bar the door. Not ready to go back upstairs, she went behind the steps into a little alcove and sat against the wall. She took a deep breath. Her head was full of questions: Who was the man? How did he know about

Thorston? Why was he interested in that blank book? Why should he say he needed her? And—she suddenly recalled—that *she* needed him? Unwilling to confront such questions, she poked idly at the old mortar in the wall behind her. It crumbled with ease. I am in a hole, she thought. I should dig myself out. With a yawn she went up the steps to the second floor. The candle had gone out, leaving the room in almost complete darkness. Odo remained asleep. Thorston was in his bed as still as before, the Book Without Words by his side.

Sybil went to the window and peered out. No one was in the courtyard. With another yawn she crept to the back room and lay down on her pallet. Her thoughts drifted back to her home, the tiny, mud-encrusted village where her parents worked endlessly in sodden fields. To the food they ate—never much. To their death from illness—common enough. To her relations' refusal to take her in—ordinary. To how, alone, she tramped to Fulworth in search of food and work. The hungry days. The lonely days. How grateful she'd been when Thorston plucked her off the street to be his servant! Yet her days were empty, isolated. Have I ever really lived? she asked herself. I might as well be dead.

The monk's words—I *need you*—came back to her. She tried to remember if anyone had ever said such a thing to her before. She could not.

Why would a perfect stranger say such a thing?

12

In another part of Fulworth, along the polluted, weed-infested, slick and slimy waters of the River Scrogg, was the tavern known as the Pure Hart. Its solitary room reeked of stale ale and sour sweat: its sagging floor creaked and groaned with the river's heaving flow. Upon its roof drummed a monotony of rain.

Inside, a solitary oil lamp, affixed to a rough-hewn wall, cast as much shadow as light. A lump of peat in a rusty iron brazier threw off more smoke than heat. The man who owned the tavern, a scarred old soldier, sat by the creaking doorway, leaning against the wall, his grizzled mouth agape, snoring like a winded ox. And at the other end of the room, upon one of three low, plank tables, sat Ambrose Bashcroft. Standing opposite him was the boy: Alfric.

"Now, then, Alfric," said Bashcroft, "you are aware, are you not, that God put children on earth to serve their adult masters?"

Alfric nodded.

"Who was that monk I bought you from?"

"I don't know, sir."

"It doesn't matter. As Fulworth's city reeve, I am your sole master now. Those who disobey me, I hang high—and often."

"Yes, sir."

"*Dura lex, sed lex.* The law is hard, but it is the law. Since I am the law, I must be hard." The reeve adjusted his bulging bulk as he leaned forward. "But, Alfric"— the reeve jabbed a hard, fat forefinger upon the boy's pigeon chest—"if you do what I say—though I paid two whole pennies for you—you'll soon be free to starve at your own convenience. There's always heaven."

"I pray so," whispered the boy. Listening to the rain beat upon the roof, he reminded himself he *was* better off inside.

"Then we understand each other," said the reeve. He peered around to make sure the innkeeper remained asleep before continuing, in a lower voice. "Now, then, Alfric, pay close heed: there's a man in town—a very old man—who goes by the name of Thorston. He's an alchemist. Which is to say, he makes—*gold.*"

"Please, sir, how does he do that?"

"That, Alfric, is something *you* must discover."

"*Me,* sir?"

"Since gold making is illegal, only I—who am the law—should know of it, so as to protect the public from its misuse. Now, then, as I say, this Master Thorston is old and dying. But, Alfric, hearken, he's in need of . . . a green-eyed boy."

Alfric lowered his eyes.

"Indeed," pronounced Bashcroft, "I never would have purchased such a worthless boy as you unless you *had* green eyes."

"My eyes can read, sir."

"Who taught you?" snapped the reeve.

"My father, sir."

"Where is he?"

"Dead, sir."

"Then reading didn't profit him much, did it?"

Alfric gave a dismal nod.

"And your mother?"

"Dead, too."

"I can assure you," said Bashcroft, "they're better off. Now then, tomorrow morning, I shall bring you to this Master Thorston's house. You will insinuate yourself into his household, discover the man's gold-making method, and deliver it to me—*only* to me."

"What will this man do with me, sir?"

"I neither know nor care. I merely warn you that if you fail to learn his secret, I'll thrash you—mercilessly. Do you understand?"

Alfric nodded.

"Moreover, I shall always be close, watching. You'll not escape me, Alfric, not until you've provided me—

50

only me—with the gold-making secret. And, if you reveal his secret to anyone else but me, I shall wring your neck like the runty puppy you are. Can you grasp that?"

"Yes, sir."

"Then you may have just enough intelligence to survive. Now, follow me." So saying, the reeve heaved himself up, wrapped himself in a great cape, and strode loudly out of the Pure Hart and into the pelting rain.

Miserable, cold, and wet, Alfric kept close.

CHAPTER THREE

1

MORNING, however unwilling, seeped into Fulworth. A gray, raw morning, with blustery winds blowing through the narrow streets and alleys, spreading the stink of rot, open privies, and spoiled food. When the bells of Saint Osyth's cathedral rang for Prime, they did so with peals that sounded like colliding lumps of lead. And in the decaying stone house at the end of Clutterbuck Lane, Sybil, through chattering teeth said, "I don't think Master wishes to live."

"He once told me," said Odo, "that when he knew he was going to die, he'd make sure he stayed alive. Like most humans, he's not kept his word."

Sybil, contemplating Thorston's unmoving face, said, "How old do you think he is?"

"Eighty years or so."

"I suppose," said Sybil, "he should be content: he's lived far longer than most."

"I don't care how long he's lived," said Odo. "I ask for just one hour—if he talks."

Sybil filled the wooden spoon with broth and continued trying to force liquid through Thorston's clenched lips. A few drops got in. Most dribbled down his chin. She wiped the spill with a dirty rag. "It's useless," she said. "He won't take anything."

"Which means *we* won't get anything," croaked the bird.

Upset, Sybil carried the bowl to the brazier where she had kept a small fire burning with chips of sea coal. Next to the fire stood the iron pot with which Thorston had been working when he took ill. She stood close to it. As she shifted about, trying to warm herself, she caught a sudden, furtive glance from Odo.

Sensing he was troubled by her nearness to the pot, she decided to look at it closely. As she bent over it she saw—out of the corner of her eye—Odo become more agitated.

She pulled back. He relaxed. She went forward. He tensed.

"Odo," she asked, certain it was her nearness to the

pot that was upsetting him, "did you ever—for a certainty—know if Master actually *made* gold?"

When the raven gave no answer, she moved her hand toward the pot.

"Sybil!" shrilled the bird.

She looked about.

"Perhaps," said Odo, "I should have told you before: I think Master found the way to make gold. In fact, I believe he was making it when he had his stroke."

"What makes you say that?"

"He cried out," said the raven, "as I never heard before. It's what woke me. Come here, and I'll describe it."

Sybil, convinced Odo was trying to keep her from the pot, did not move. "Odo, if Master did make gold it should be about. Could it be—in here?" She gestured toward the pot.

The bird bobbed his head up and down. "You may be assured I've looked. It's not there."

Sybil felt a surge of anger. "When did you look?"

"When I discovered him ill."

"And what, Master raven, did you find?"

"I told you, nothing."

"Is that when you woke me?" cried Sybil. "Only *after* you found nothing?" Furious, she plunged her hand into the pot.

"Don't!" screamed the bird.

Sybil worked her fingers through the thick, pongy

mess. Touching some lumps, she cried, "Odo, there *is* something."

"Gold?" cried the bird. He hopped toward her.

Sybil snatched up the lumps, and turned from him.

"Is it gold?" repeated Odo, beating about her. "Is it?"

Keeping her back to the bird, Sybil wiped the lumps on her gown and looked at them. There were three of them, greenish, imperfectly round, each smaller than the next, the smallest the size of a pea. "They are only stones," she said, with a sinking heart. "Green ones."

"Show them to me!" squawked Odo as he jumped to her arm and gave her a sharp peck. Sybil, clutching the stones in one hand, smacked the bird away with the other.

Odo glared up at her from the floor. "Idiot!"

Sybil, annoyed by the bird, went to the foot of the bed, where a wooden chest sat upon the floor. She knelt. Trusting the lid screened her movements, she put the stones beneath a bolt of cloth, then took up a small leather pouch—Thorston's money pouch. She let the chest lid slam shut and drew out the few coins that were inside. "What will give out first—Master, the money—or us?"

"What difference will a few coins make?" spat out the raven. "All you've insured is that *our* deaths will closely follow his." He shook his head, jumped to the window, and peered out through the glass, tail feathers twitching with agitation. Suddenly he croaked, "Sybil— a boy is coming here."

2

"Are you certain?" cried Sybil, forgetting about the stones.

"Where else could he be going?" said Odo. "There's no other house but ours in this horrid court. God's mercy! He's with the city reeve."

"Master Bashcroft?"

"Yes! He's pushing the boy—who doesn't seem eager to move—forward. Now the reeve has retreated. But not far. He's shaking a fist at the lad."

"Does the boy have green eyes?"

"Sybil, I don't care if he's entirely green. If it's Bashcroft who's sending him, we should have nothing to do with him."

Sybil opened the chest, threw back Thorston's pouch, slammed the lid back down, and stood up. "But green eyes are what I need," she said. She took up the candle and headed for the steps.

"Are you truly going to let him in?" Odo screeched after her.

"I am," said Sybil, "but things will go badly if he hears you talk."

She hurried to the ground floor just in time to hear a timid knock on the door.

"Who's there?" she called.

"Please, I'm a child," said a small voice. "With green eyes. I'm here to see Master Thorston."

Sybil looked around at Odo, who had followed her down the steps. "There," she said, "my plan worked."

"Alas! But you mustn't let him in."

Enjoying the raven's frustration, Sybil removed the crossbeam and pulled in the heavy door.

Alfric stood on the threshold, his head bowed so that Sybil could see nothing of his eyes. She could see his unruly red hair, his ragged clothing, his torn boots, and that he was younger than she.

"Please, Mistress," said Alfric, speaking in a whisper and addressing the ground, "I was told a boy with green eyes was wanted." His trembling fingers—raw with cold—twisted in distress.

"Who told you?" said Sybil.

"Master Bashcroft." Alfric turned halfway around.

Sybil followed his gaze but saw no one in the courtyard. "Let me see your eyes."

A reluctant Alfric lifted his head. Tears were running down his red, chapped face.

"God's grace, boy," said Sybil. "What ails you?"

"I'm frightened."

"Of what?"

"Of what will happen to me here." He covered his face with his hands as if to ward off a blow.

Gently, Sybil pulled the boy's hand away and looked at his eyes anew. Seeing that they were green, her heart fluttered. "By all grace," she said, "nothing bad shall befall you here. Step in."

When Alfric edged forward, Sybil shut the door behind him. The noise made the boy jump.

"May I know your name?" said Sybil as she set back the crossbar.

"Alfric," the boy said with a shuddering sob. "Please, Mistress, I didn't want to find out about how to make the gold."

"Gold?" said a startled Sybil. "What gold?"

"That your master makes."

Sybil heard Odo hiss softly. To Alfric she said, "You appear hungry. Are you?"

"Yes, please."

"Come. I'll give you something warm." She turned toward the steps.

The boy hesitated.

"I shan't hurt you," said Sybil. "It's only your green eyes that are wanted."

The boy threw himself back up against the door. "Are you going to cut them out?" he cried.

58

"No, no! You need only *look* at something with them," said Sybil. She moved toward the steps, turning to make sure Alfric was coming.

Halfway up the steps they passed Odo who fixed his beady eyes on the boy. Alfric shied away but continued on. When he reached the gloomy room, he stopped and looked about, wide-eyed.

Odo went to his customary roost upon the skull.

"Mistress," the boy whispered, "is that old man . . . dead?"

"Just resting," said Sybil. She drew the three-legged stool close to the hot brazier. "Pray sit," she said.

Alfric, sitting on the stool's edge, looked about the room. Now and again he wiped his face with his dirty hands.

Sybil placed the bowl from which she had been attempting to feed Thorston back on the brazier. As it warmed, she watched Alfric survey the room. She sensed he was looking for something.

"Tell me, Alfric," she said, "what is your connection to Master Bashcroft?"

"He bought me for two pennies."

"Bought you! Where are your parents, then?"

"Dead," the boy whispered.

"May they find grace," said Sybil as she handed the bowl to the boy.

With a look of gratitude, Alfric took the bowl in

both raw hands. He allowed himself a sip; then a second, deeper one. His third swallow drained the bowl. Though the bowl was empty, he continued to clutch it, reluctant to give up its warmth.

"Now, Alfric," said Sybil, "I require you to look at something with those green eyes of yours."

"Mistress, I can read. Truly. My father, who did ledgers for merchants, was also a scrivener. He taught me the skill."

"Even better," said Sybil, glancing at Odo and feeling a heart swell of anticipation. She went to Thorston's bed, took up the Book Without Words, placed it on Alfric's knees, and opened it at random. "Be so good as to read what you see."

As Alfric bent over the open page, Odo hopped closer to observe better. Sybil also watched intently.

After a long time Alfric looked up. "Please, Mistress," he whispered. "There are no words here."

Sybil sighed. "Turn some pages. Perhaps you'll find something."

Alfric reached the end of the book. "I don't see anything," he said. "Is it something I've done?"

Even as he spoke there came a loud pounding on the door below.

3

Sybil looked to Odo. The raven's head was up, bright black eyes full of alarm.

"It must be Master Bashcroft," whispered Alfric. His thin chest heaved. Tears began to flow. "He said he'd be watching me closely. Said he'd beat me if I don't find out how your master makes gold."

Odo jumped up to the window and peered down. Sybil joined him.

"Now what do you propose to do?" the bird whispered.

"Look there," said Sybil, tapping the glass with her finger. "In that far doorway. It's Bashcroft. So it can't be him who's knocking."

"No doubt," said Odo, "he's sending an army of green-eyed children."

Sybil turned to boy. "Alfric," she called, "did you come with anyone beside the reeve?"

Alfric, his face full of fright, was standing stiff as a stick with the Book Without Words clutched to his chest like a shield. He shook his head.

Another knock came.

Sybil gave Odo a warning look, as if to say "Don't

speak!" then hastened down the steps, candle in hand. By the time she reached the seventh step, Odo had leaped to her shoulder, and he rode the rest of the way down with her. He pecked her neck twice, but she ignored it.

"Who's there?" she called when she reached the door.

"A child with green eyes," was the bellowed reply from the other side. "Here to see Master Thorston."

"God's grace," said Sybil, "whoever it is, he doesn't lack for boldness." She pulled the door open.

On the threshold stood Damian.

Sybil, recognizing him as the apothecary's apprentice, was immediately alarmed. She took a mental measure of him. He was bigger than she, well fed, but not much older. She noted his pimpled red face and the fact that he wore decent boots and a wool jacket. He seemed soft, with much padding.

"I am Damian Perbeck. Apprentice to Mistress Weebly, the apothecary. My eyes are green."

Despite feeling an instant dislike for the boy, Sybil stepped aside. "Enter," she said.

Damian eyed her. "Who are you?"

"Master Thorston's servant."

"Then my business is not with you," said the boy. He stepped inside and turned his back on her. "Take me to your master."

"I'll take you nowhere, till you tell me why you've come," said Sybil as she slammed the door, set the bar, and faced the boy.

"Mistress Weebly, knowing Master Thorston is in need of a green-eyed child, sent me. To learn his alchemy."

Odo glared at Damian from Sybil's shoulder. Damian, eyeing the bird with disgust, folded his arms over his chest. "I'll answer you no more," he said. "Lead the way."

4

Spying into the courtyard from Clutterbuck Lane, Bashcroft could not believe what he had just seen: Damian Perbeck, Mistress Weebly's apprentice, entering the alchemist's house. Could that boy have green eyes too? Did that mean the apothecary was after the gold for herself?

Selfish wench. How dare she!

"*Dura lex, sed lex,*" the reeve murmured. Then he swore an oath that he would wait and watch until doomsday if required. Indeed, to get that gold, he would hang them all.

5

Damian, following Sybil, reached the top step and gazed about the jumbled room. "Ah!" he exclaimed when he spied the old man. "Is this Master Thorston, the alchemist?" He went to the bedside. "What ails him?"

"He's sleeping."

"Wake him and tell him I'm here."

"I'll do no such thing," said Sybil.

"Then why are my green eyes wanted?" said Damian. "Who is this disgusting boy? Why is that dirty bird here?"

Instead of answering, Sybil went to Alfric and took the Book Without Words from him.

"Pray, sit," she said to Damian.

Damian glared at her. "And if I don't?"

"Then you may leave. Now."

"What is it you wish of me?" he said.

"We require a reading. Can you do it?"

"Of course," said Damian. "My tutor taught me."

"Then sit."

"I sit because I choose to," said Damian as he sat, "not because you tell me."

Sybil put the book on his lap. "Read this," she said.

Damian contemplated a few pages. After a while he looked up. "Is this some kind of joke?" he said. "There's nothing here to read. If you would just tell me your master's gold-making secrets, I'll be pleased to go." He snapped the book shut and stood up.

Sybil didn't know what to say.

"May I remind you," said Damian, "I'm Mistress Weebly's apprentice. As the town apothecary, she's very powerful. Accordingly, know that I too am powerful."

When Sybil only stared at him, the boy flushed and added: "In some ways, at least."

Sybil snatched the book out of Damian's hands and carried it to the bed. "Master," she shouted, as if he were deaf, "we have two people with green eyes! They see nothing! Tell us what to do!"

When the old man made no response, Odo fluttered across the room and landed on the bed. Head cocked to one side, he studied the alchemist intently.

"Master," Sybil cried again. "Speak to us. What shall we do?"

Odo hopped the length of the bed. Leaning forward, he stared fixedly at Thorston's inert face, cocking his head first one way then another. "Sybil," he said, "he's not going to answer. Ever. Master Thorston is dead."

6

Tightness came to Sybil's chest. It was hard for her to breathe. Her head hurt. "God's mercy," she managed to whisper.

"Dead," croaked the raven, his eyes blinking rapidly. "Gone to wherever treacherous men such as he belong. We are lost!"

Alfric and Damian gaped. "Did . . . did that bird *talk*?" asked Damian.

Odo, paying no heed, kept muttering, "Doomed. Cut off. Abandoned." He leaped closer to the dead man's face. "Cruel Master," he croaked, "did you forget your promise? Now the reeve will discover your death. But it's *we* who shall lose everything." Livid, he pecked the old man's nose.

"Stop that," cried Sybil. "Have you no respect?"

"Respect!" cried Odo. "What respect had he for me? Or you, for that matter? None. He treated all with contempt. How long did I put up with him! What do I have for my pains?" he screeched. "*Nothing*. Less than nothing."

"That raven," said Alfric, "he's truly talking."

"Doesn't he know," said Damian, "it's unnatural for beasts to talk?"

Odo leaned toward Sybil. "Idiot!" he screamed. "I warned you. Now what do you propose to do?"

"That talking is magic, isn't it?" said Damian. Nervous, he moved toward the steps

Sybil whirled about. "Anyone can talk," she cried. "You talk. I have yet to hear you say one intelligent word. Does that make you a bird?"

Damian's face turned bright red. "You have no right to speak to me that way," he said. "I'm your superior."

"Does your master's death mean that you don't want me anymore?" said Alfric. "That I must go?"

"Come here, both of you," Sybil snapped at the boys.

The two eyed one another. Alfric came forward. Damian stood his ground. "What for?" he demanded.

"It's gold!" shouted Sybil, her frustration bursting forth. "The secret of gold-making is in this book. But Master told us it can only be read by someone with green eyes." She flung the book on the table. Some of the apparatus flew off and smashed.

"God in heaven," screamed Odo. "You've told them."

"Well, then," said Damian, a smile on his lips, "if *that's* what it is, perhaps I may be of use." He swaggered forward. Pushing Alfric aside, he bent over the book. After a few silent moments he looked up. "Nonsense," he said. "There's still nothing here. Nothing."

"You try," Sybil said to Alfric.

Alfric wiped his face with his grubby fingers and leaned over the pages, staring hard. In a few moments he looked up. "Please, Mistress, there's nothing more than last time."

"Fooled," screeched Odo. "Tricked. Deceived."

Sybil, biting her lip to keep from screaming, went to the window and stared out. Bashcroft was lurking in a doorway, moving his feet up and down, beating his chest with his hands to keep warm.

"If your master," Damian announced, "is dead, there's little point in my staying. Anyway, there's something grossly unnatural here. A dead man. A bird that talks." He smirked. "There is nothing to stay for. I am leaving." He moved toward the stairs.

"If you go," said Sybil without looking at him, "I won't share any of Master's magic with you."

Odo, opening his beak with surprise, looked around at Sybil from the bed.

"Ah!" said Damian, grinning. "Then you do know magic. I thought as much."

"Of course I know *magic*," cried Sybil, so upset she didn't care what she said. She was glaring out the window, arms folded over her chest. "Haven't I been the alchemist's servant for . . . *years*? How could I not learn his secrets?" She turned to face him. "You may think I am nothing." She gulped back tears. "I may not have been his kin, but he treated me with . . . great kindness. *Love*."

"I don't care how he treated you," said Damian. "I'll stay, but only if you show me some of your magic."

Sybil darted a panicky look at Odo, who was sitting on Thorston's head. He shrugged, lifted a claw, and muttered, "*Risan . . . risan.*" Next moment, the skull—Odo's customary perch—rose into the air a few feet. Momentarily, it hovered, only to drop and shatter into bits.

As the boys stared with amazement Sybil darted a ferocious look at Odo. But after taking a deep breath, she turned to Damian and said, "There, you see, *my* magic. Now you are perfectly free to leave."

"Did you truly do that?" exclaimed Damian, who had been watching Sybil, not Odo.

"Who else would?" said Sybil. Unwilling to look at Odo, she spun about and stared out the window. "And when you leave," she called, "be free to greet Master Bashcroft. He's waiting right outside."

"Bashcroft?" said Damian. "Out there?"

"He watched you as you came."

The boy paled. "He did? The reeve is the most despicable man in Fulworth," he said. "I'll have nothing to do with him."

"He seems to be spying on you," said Sybil.

"Please, Mistress," said Alfric, "Let me stay. I'll do whatever you ask. Just don't send me back to that man."

Damian shoved Sybil aside and looked down into

the courtyard at the reeve. "He bullies Mistress Weebly," he said. "Which makes her bully me."

"Sybil," said Odo, "may I remind you: if Bashcroft discovers Master is dead, he will walk right in and take possession of everything. Including us."

"Can't you do something to keep him away?" Damian said to Sybil. "You're a magician."

Sybil peered down into the courtyard before turning back to Odo. "There is something we can do: we can bury him."

"*Bury the city reeve?*" cried Odo.

"Don't be silly," said Sybil. "Bury Master Thorston."

7

"What are you saying?" shrieked Odo.

"Did I not say it simply enough?" said Sybil. "We must bury Master in the cellar."

"In the *cellar*?" cried Damian.

"Have you a cemetery there?" asked Alfric.

"But why?" said Odo.

"Because if we take Master's body out of the building, his death will be noted—will it not?"

"Yes, but—"

"If his death is noted," Sybil continued, "you said so yourself—we'll lose all chance of learning anything. Bury him here, and no one need know. It will give us time to find his secrets."

"May I remind you," said Damian, "I did see him die. Anyway, you can't just bury a person in one's house. It must be in sacred ground."

Sybil glared at him. "You're perfectly welcome to leave," she said. "This has nothing to do with you."

"It has everything to do with me," returned Damian. "I've come to learn your master's secrets. You've made it clear you have some. I've no intention of leaving without learning them."

Knocking erupted on the front door.

"God's mercy," cried Odo. "If that's another green-eyed child, I shall lie on my back and stick my feet into the air."

Sybil, seeing Damian wince, said, "What are you frightened about?"

"It's possibly my mistress come after me."

"Why should she do that?"

"I've . . . I've run away."

Alfric, who had been looking out the window, said, "Please, I think it's Master Bashcroft."

"That's no better," said Damian.

"This boy belongs to him," said Sybil, pointing to Alfric.

Damian looked on Alfric as if for the first time. "What do you mean *belongs* to him?"

Alfric hung his head. "He bought me."

There was more pounding on the door.

"Please, Mistress," said Alfric, tugging on Sybil's sleeve. "I want to stay."

"You may stay," said Sybil. "But you, Master Damian, decide: Go or stay?"

"I can't go home," said Damian, "I have to have the secrets."

The knocking below resumed.

"Well?" said Sybil.

"I'll stay."

"Good," said Sybil. "Then I'll deal with the reeve."

Sybil hurried down the stairs. As she did, Odo leaped to her shoulder.

"You did that, didn't you?" said Sybil.

"Did what?"

"Made that skull rise."

"I did only what you requested."

"Master raven, how many of Master's secrets do you know?"

"Sybil, if you truly are going to bury Master here, I promise you that Damian will spread the news. Things will go badly."

"Master Odo, since you won't answer my questions and only change the subject, I intend to take care of myself." As she reached for the door, it suddenly occurred to her that the ancient monk—the one she met the night before—might be on the other side. "Who is it?" she called.

"It's I, Ambrose Bashcroft, the reeve of Fulworth. *Dura lex, sed lex.* The law is hard, but it is the law. Since I am the law, I must see Master Thorston."

"In faith, sir," called Sybil, "my master is in no condition to have visitors."

"To whom am I speaking?"

"His servant, sir."

"Why can't your master have visitors?"

Sybil looked over her shoulder. Alfric and Damian had come down the steps. "Master Reeve," she cried through the closed door. "My master's condition is such that he will speak to no one."

"Dying, is he? Then I'll speak to my boy, Alfric. Send him out immediately."

"But, sir," called Sybil, "even as you speak, your boy is about to attend my master."

There was a moment of silence, after which the reeve said, "What is he doing?"

"He is going to help my master find his rest."

"Is your master talking to him?"

"I've no doubt your boy is listening to every word my master utters."

"Very well," said the reeve. "I'll return on the morrow at noon. I'll speak to your master then. Advise him that I've ample reason to believe that dangerous doings are being conducted in this house."

"I shall tell him," said Sybil. She pressed an ear to the door. "He's gone," she announced after a moment.

"But he'll be back," cried Odo.

"Then," said Sybil, "we'd best bury Master quickly."

9

Sybil knelt by the trapdoor, grasped its iron rung, and yanked. It barely gave.

Odo started to lift a claw but stopped himself.

"Come here," Sybil called to the boys. "I need your help."

Alfric took hold of the ring. "Blessings on you for letting me stay," he whispered.

"By God's hands, you're most welcome," said Sybil. "Just lift." The two pulled. With a jerk, the trapdoor came up, exposing a square, dark hole.

"Are there more dead below?" asked Damian.

"Don't be a fool," said Sybil. "There's nothing but dirt."

"You call me a fool, but it's clear you have no respect for the dead," said Damian.

"Whereas you have no respect for the living," returned Sybil. "Now, come," she said. "Both of you. We need to work in haste."

She sat on the square's open edge. A rickety ladder led into the dark. She started down. The air was damp, cold, and smelled horrible. The basement had a dirt floor, and nothing was there save for two old chests with rusty locks. It had been so long since Sybil had gone into the basement, she had forgotten about them.

Odo dropped onto her shoulder. "This is madness," he hissed. "Why are you doing this?"

"Odo," Sybil returned in a hushed voice, "tell me the secrets you learned from our master, or by Saint Osyth, I'll wring your neck and bury you by his side."

"What do you mean?" cried the alarmed bird.

"It's perfectly clear," said Sybil, "you know some of Master's magic. That skull rising was proof enough."

"You may be sure *he* never taught me," said the raven. "I had to spy on him."

"Why did you let the skull break?"

"I didn't *let* it. It's what his magic seems to do: something good happens, then . . . the opposite."

"What other magic did you learn?"

"A few pretty things."

"Such as?"

"I . . . I can make small objects rise up in the air. But little beyond my own weight."

"And?"

"I can move . . . *things*—as I did with the skull. But just for short distances. And either they go back where they came from—or they break."

"Nothing more?"

"Sometimes I can turn hard objects—again, puny ones—into water. It's useful when I'm thirsty."

"Go on."

"God's truth, there is no more."

"I'm not sure I believe you."

"What you believe doesn't matter," said the bird. "What will we do when the reeve returns?"

"I'll deal with him then," said Sybil.

"Have you no fear of death?"

"It's not my death I fear," said Sybil, "but my life. Now, go tell the boys to bring the shovels."

"Idiocy," muttered the raven as he fluttered up. But within moments Sybil heard him croak, "She says to bring the shovels."

10

It was Alfric who carried down the shovels, one with an iron blade, the other wood. Damian came next, descending clumsily, continually muttering complaints. Odo, feathers agitated, settled himself on a rung halfway down the ladder and watched. Now and again he fluttered his wings or bobbed his tail.

Damian, holding his nose, said, "It stinks like a privy here."

"Master used it so," said Sybil, "but it will serve." She took the iron shovel from Alfric and began to dig close to the foot of the ladder where the dirt was soft. Alfric worked by her side.

"I wish to announce," said Damian from the chest upon which he was sitting, "that in my whole life I've never dug anything. Certainly not a grave. I have no intention of doing so now."

Sybil, making no response, worked in silence, scooping up the sandy loam and piling it up to one side.

"It's said," Odo pronounced from the ladder rung, "the deeper the grave, the more undisturbed the death."

"You surely don't want your master to return," Damian said with a grin. "He looks most unlikable."

Sybil paused to wipe the grime and sweat from her face. "You know nothing about him."

"I suppose," Damian went on, "that whereas alchemy is illegal, the gold made is legal enough. Therefore, in payment for keeping silence about what's happening here, I will want my share."

"You are a beastly boy," said Odo, his eyes glittering.

"At least I'm human," said Damian.

"And where did Master Thorston put his hoard?" Damian said. "In here?" He thumped the chest on which he sat, and jangled the heavy, rusty lock that held it shut. When no one replied, he bent over, picked up a rock, and pounded the lock. The lock held, and the blow only stung his hand.

Sybil looked up from the grave pit. "Master Damian," she cried, "if you desire one grain of my master's gold, by God's bones, you'll keep quiet."

"Does that mean the gold *is* about?" retorted the boy.

"Of course it is," said Sybil.

Sybil and Alfric kept digging until Odo, from the ladder said; "I should think that's deep enough."

"Then it's time," said Sybil, "to put Master to his final rest."

11

They made their way to the upper room and stood by Thorston's bed. The dead man lay as they had left him: face dull white, eyes sunken, toothless mouth agape, body somewhat shrunken within his blue robe. His knobby, motionless hands rested by his sides.

"I admit," said Sybil as she gazed at him, "I don't care for this. He may have been unpleasant, but it's not easy to think him dead."

"You said he treated you kindly," said Damian.

"Death gives life to memories," Odo said.

"Mistress," Alfric whispered, "are you quite certain he's gone?"

Odo hopped onto the old man's body, lowered his head to Thorston's chest, and listened. "Nothing remains but his mortal husk," he proclaimed.

"His purse," said Damian. "You're not going to bury that, are you?"

"It's not wise to remove anything from a dead man," returned Sybil. "Indeed, his old blanket can be his winding sheet." Holding her breath, she leaned across the corpse, snatched up his blanket, drew it over his body, and covered him head to toe.

"A sexton should be doing this," said Damian. "Or some old woman from the church, whose duty it is to lay bodies out. And there should be a priest."

Sybil, ignoring the boy, said, "I'll lift him. When I do, best tuck it under." She braced herself, then plunged her arms under the body and lifted, taken aback by how light he was. "He's not heavy," she said. "Does a soul weigh so much?"

"I've heard say," said Damian, "the more one sins the heavier one gets."

"No wonder you are gross," said Odo.

"Slanderer."

Alfric tucked the blanket under, after which Sybil lowered the body. Thorston looked like a rolled-up rug.

"Now we must carry him down," said Sybil. Her voice trembled.

"You made that skull rise," said Damian. "Can't you make him float down?"

Sybil darted a glance at Odo.

The bird, standing atop Thorston's chest, gave a tiny shake of his head. "I shall direct this," he said. "Sybil, take his shoulders. Damian, his feet. Alfric, hoist the middle."

Sybil, trying to keep from being sick, put her hands under Thorston's shoulders and jerked up. The body farted.

"He lives!" cried Damian, bursting into laughter.

"Stop your mockery," said Sybil, trying to keep from laughing, too.

There were a few stumbles, but no one lost their grip, though Damian wheezed from his efforts.

"Go slower," said Sybil. "Or I'll fall." She took a step down, backward. The others pushed. "Not so fast." she cried, barely managing to keep from tumbling.

"This is the most dreadful thing I've ever done in my life," said Damian.

"Death is part of life," Odo snapped.

Sybil continued downward one step at a time—backward. Once, twice, she teetered and called out, "Careful!" When she did, Alfric pushed up from below. It brought on another body fart.

"God's miracles," cried Damian, "we should be taking him to a privy, not his grave."

Amid more laughter they reached the lower floor.

Once there, Sybil shifted the body so that Thorston's lolling head was close to the trapdoor. She moved down the ladder, pausing a third of the way.

"Lower him," she called up to the others as she braced herself. "I'll keep him from tumbling."

Grunting and grumbling, Alfric and Damian did as told. The body edged over the hole headfirst, then went down toward Sybil's reaching arms.

"Blessed Lord!" she screamed. "He's falling!"

Thorston's corpse slid down the ladder—*bump,*

bump—over the rungs, and dropped at the ladder's foot directly into the grave, with a heavy *thump*.

They scrambled down the ladder after him. Sybil snatched up the candle, and, heart pounding, peered into the grave. "God's mercy," she said.

"This is almost farcical," said Damian, grinning broadly.

"When you are older," said Odo, "you'll learn that farce is but tragedy in excess."

Alfric peered into the grave. "He's all twisted."

"Straighten him out," Damian said to Sybil.

Sybil, though irritated the boy was giving her orders, climbed into the grave.

"Don't step on him!" cried Odo.

Trying to keep from gagging, Sybil aligned Thorston's body so that he lay reasonably straight.

"Now what?" said Damian when Sybil had hauled herself out.

"He must be covered by earth," said Odo.

"Shall I speak what was said over my parents' grave?" asked Alfric.

"It would be kind," said Sybil.

Alfric took a deep breath and then said, "Rest in peace."

There was a moment of awkward silence. "Surely," cried Damian, "there was more said."

"That's all the priest spoke," said Alfric.

82

"Never mind," said Sybil, feeling ill. "We must finish." With Alfric's help, she started to shovel dirt over the body. As she did, she began to cry. Odo bobbed his head with grief. Alfric wept, too.

"Why are you crying?" Damian asked Alfric.

"I'm thinking of my parents."

"Being without parents hardly makes you special," said Damian. "I'm an orphan, too."

"As am I," said Sybil through a sob. "And Odo."

"Live long enough," said Odo, "and all become orphans."

Damian looked around. "It's a mercy your sermons are short," he said.

"My father," said Alfric, "was wont to say, 'The shorter the sermon, the longer the truth.'"

Sybil stepped back and wiped her hands on her frock.

"Are we finished?" said Damian.

"Yes," whispered Sybil, without strength to speak louder.

"Then I want my reward," said Damian. "And I want it now. Or I shall immediately go to the reeve. I'm sure he will be pleased to know what you've done."

12

"Go up to the room," said Sybil, "and wait. I need to talk to Odo." Alfric went. Damian did not.

"Why can't you speak with me here?" he said.

"Just go!" Sybil cried.

Damian, seeing the fierceness of Sybil's face, climbed the ladder without further protest.

As soon as they were alone, a nervous Odo said, "What did you wish to say?"

"Even with their green eyes," Sybil whispered, "the boys can make nothing of that book. What are we to do?"

"I don't know," admitted Odo.

"I wish," said Sybil, looking the bird in the eyes, "I could trust you more."

"You can."

"Then tell me about Master. If I knew more about him, I might understand more about the gold. Odo, what kind of man was he?"

"What does it matter? Dead men do few deeds."

"How long were you with him?"

The bird hung his head. "I'm not sure."

"How can that be?"

Odo nodded a few time before saying, "Sybil, the truth

is, I suspect I was something else before I was a raven."

"What do you mean?" said Sybil.

"I believe Master transformed me from something else."

"Was he a sorcerer, then?"

"Of a kind. And in transforming me, he also took my memory."

"Could he truly have done all that?"

"All his magic came from the book."

"Then have you *no* idea what you were?"

"I'd like to think I was a human," said the raven. "But, for all I know I could have been a . . . cabbage. Or a goat. Master always liked goats."

"But why would he want you to be a raven?"

"I suspect it has something to do with the making of gold. At least, he promised me half the gold he made if I would stay with him and let him use my feathers. I even allowed him to clip my wings—my foolish way of assuring him I wouldn't fly away. Sybil, he told me there was a man in York who could restore my wings so I could fly again. Of course, it would take gold; but I supposed I'd have a great deal."

"Odo, is flying all you seek?"

The raven dropped down a rung closer to the girl. "Sybil, look at me. I'm an old, useless bird. Unable to fly, I'm bound to this wretched earth. I talk only to you, an impoverished peasant girl. What a pair. I cannot fly—you are ignorant. Have you no desires?"

"You always say I'm nothing," said Sybil. "Perhaps it's true. But all the same, I want to live, though I can't say for what purpose. Perhaps being alive is enough. Odo, it was you who convinced me Master's gold-making secret could make a difference in my life. Now all we have are those stones. I put them in the chest."

"I suspected as much," said the bird. "I wish I knew their importance. But I still think we can find gold."

"Then," said Sybil, "are we agreed? Even though there appear to be no secrets to be learned from that book, we must make these boys stay, if only to keep the news of Master's death a secret. We'll use the time for searching. Have you no idea what's in these chests?"

"None."

Sybil saw the rock that Damian had used, and used it to strike the locks hard, one after the other. They held. "Have you ever seen keys?" she asked.

"Never."

"Perhaps it's magic that keeps them closed. But we need to look for keys, too." She glanced at the grave. "Oh, Odo, at least Master is dead and gone. They say it's wrong to speak ill of the dead. But if ever there were a more unpleasant man, 'twas he. A sullen, angry man. And he treated us poorly."

"And yet," said Odo, "if by gaining our freedom from him we lose our lives, what have we won?"

Sybil shrugged. "Sometimes I think I've never done anything that could be called true living."

"Gold!" cried the bird. "Put your faith in that!" And he went up the ladder.

Sybil looked at the Thorston's grave. Suddenly she remembered: the old monk had spoken of the Book Without Words. And he knew of Master. She made up her mind that if she had the opportunity, she would ask him more.

13

When Sybil reached the upper room, Alfric was by the window gazing out. Damian was sitting on the stool. The moment she appeared he said, "How long do you expect me to stay?"

"Until we find gold," said Sybil.

"We believe," said Odo, "our master hid his gold somewhere—here about."

"Mid this disarray?" said Damian.

"Yes," said Odo.

Damian stood up. "But if I stay, I have no intention of working."

"So be it," said Sybil, and she offered up a silent prayer of relief.

The search began. Sybil set Alfric the task of finding all small bottles and placing them on the table, which he was happy to do. She tried to set the room into better order by dumping pieces of glass and debris in one corner, collecting useless items in another, putting Thorston's alchemic apparatus upright. The only thing she did not touch—sensing it was important—was the pot from which she had taken the stones. Odo busied himself by fluttering about, peering everywhere, poking into the small things he could grasp in his beak or talons.

Damian, true to his word, sat on Thorston's bed and merely watched. But as the day wore on he became bored. In time he began to help—if only in a half-hearted way.

By early evening, the room was in far better order, the stench less odious. Even so, nothing of importance had been found. So when the cathedral bells rang for Vespers, a weary Sybil fetched a fist of barley from the back room along with a half cabbage and some turnips so they might eat.

"Water," she reminded herself. It had always been her chore to fetch it from the well. Without even considering that anyone else might do the task, she took up a wooden bucket and went down the steps to the ground floor and opened the door. After checking to make sure no one was lurking about, she stepped away from the house.

14

Sybil darted across the courtyard, going directly to the well. Once there, feeling a vague unease, she looked about. A low fog lay like a shallow swamp upon the ground, rendering the courtyard formless—as if it were there but not there. It made her think of Master Thorston in his grave—here—but *not* here.

As Sybil tried to imagine death, she tied the well rope to her bucket handle and flung it down. It landed with a distant splash.

Is death—she found herself thinking—like an empty bucket at the bottom of a well?

Even as she had the thought, the bucket settled and filled. She began to haul it up. Is that what life is? A full bucket, rising? Then where am I? she asked herself—rising or falling?

"I want to rise," she said aloud.

Her musing faded when, with a start, she became aware that someone had entered the courtyard. She looked up. It was Brother Wilfrid. As he drew to within a few feet of her she became frightened but made herself hold fast.

The monk halted. His green eyes, amid the mass of face wrinkles, fixed upon her. "You are fearful of me," he said.

"I am," said Sybil.

"You need not be. I'm little more than a presence with neither the strength nor inclination to do you harm. There are more important people to fear than me."

"Who?"

"Thorston."

"He's dead," said Sybil.

"Dead!"

"We buried him today."

"Where?"

"In the house," said Sybil, belatedly thinking she should not have made the admission.

Brother Wilfrid seemed to sway in a breeze. "Did he . . . did he not make the stones?" he asked.

Though she knew exactly what the monk was asking about, Sybil said, "What stones?"

"He was making them when I first came," said Wilfrid. "They must be in the house. You need to find them. You are in great danger."

"Why?"

"Do you know nothing about them?"

Sybil shook her head.

Brother Wilfrid was silent for a long moment. "Then you must hear me," he finally said.

15

"It was in 973," began the monk, "seventy-three years ago, that a boy was born. Extraordinary omens occurred: stars fell out of the heavens. On Saint Waccar's day, the sun grew dark at noon. Sheets of fire hung in the night sky. Between cockcrow and dawn, frightful flashes of lightning were observed. There were those who swore they had seen dragons flying through the air. These dreadful omens were followed by a great famine that stirred the flames of civil conflict. All over Northumbria, thieves and brigands roamed. In the strife that followed, the boy's parents were killed.

"Relations took the child in, but the ravages of famine overwhelmed all, and he lost them, too. Alone, he lived in fear. And when it appeared as if life could not be worse, news spread that Viking raiders had returned to Northumbria. They looted churches and slaughtered many, while taking some into slavery and holding others for ransom.

"Devastation ruled the land.

"So it was that by the time the boy reached thirteen years of age, beyond all else, he feared death.

"The boy heard that the safest place on earth was Saint Elfleda's monastery, which was on a small island off the northeastern coast of Northumbria. There he accepted the only work he could get, that of a goatherd."

"Who was that boy?" asked Sybil.

"Your master, Thorston."

16

"One afternoon," the monk went on, "long boats with high dragon bows and long oars appeared. The boats carried some two hundred bearded, long-haired men with iron helmets, and chain mail on their chests. Shields on the boats sides proclaimed them to be Viking raiders.

"After dragging the boats high onto the beaches, the men took up axes, swords, and shields. With fierce shouts and cries, they raced inland. When the monks of Saint Elfleda's saw them, they dropped their tools and fled, only to be overtaken and killed. Screams of terror and cries for mercy filled the air. Looting began. From a place of concealment Thorston saw it all.

"How old are you?" the monk suddenly asked Sybil.

"Thirteen," she said.

"His age at that time, exactly.

"As for me, at the time I was a young monk entrusted with a great responsibility, a book. Clutching this book I fled the monastery through a small door in the wall, only to come upon a very frightened Thorston. The boy reeked of goat. 'Follow me,' I cried to him.

"The two of us ran to the western side of the island, and then over the sandbar to the mainland. Once we were safe—thinking he would help me—I foolishly told Thorston about the Book Without Words. 'You should praise God,' I told him, 'that He has sent you—as a means of your salvation—to help keep this book from evildoers.'

"'Why do you have it, then?'

"'Young and weak though I am, Abbot Sigfrid entrusted it to me that I might shield it from those who might use it,'" I said, and I opened the book and gingerly turned the stiff, yellow parchment pages.

"Thorston, looking down over my shoulder, said, 'Brother Wilfrid, the pages are blank. How does one read it?'

"'It requires green eyes and earthly desire.'

"'Why green eyes?' he asked.

"'The old religion claimed green to be the color of life.'

"'And earthly desire?'

"'The things most wanted.'

"'Brother Wilfrid,' said Thorston, 'I was once told I had green eyes.'

"I darted a look at him. When I saw that his eyes were indeed green, I became alarmed and closed the book.

"But he had become excited. 'Brother Wilfrid,' he said, 'can the book's magic tell me how to live forever?'

"I stood up. 'I must go,' I said.

"Thorston restrained me. 'Please,' he pleaded, 'my desire is never to die. Teach me how to read and use the book.'

"'No,' I said, pulling free, 'it's not for such as you and I.' But I held out my hand. 'Be my friend and companion. If something happens to me, you could bring the book to our bishop. You would be blessed.'

"'But, Brother Wilfrid, if we used the book's magic, we—'

"'Didn't you hear me?' I said. 'It must not be used. I must get it to safety. Thank you for your assistance. Godspeed,' I said, 'and a blessed death.' I started off.

"Abruptly, Thorston threw his tunic over my head, smothering me. He struck, too. As I fell, he tore the Book Without Words from my grasp, took back his tunic, and ran off through the forest.

"I lay dying on the thick forest floor, the stench of goat in my nostrils. 'Saint Elfleda,' I cried, 'help me retrieve the book.'

"And so," concluded the monk, "she has."

94

17

"Is all of that true?" whispered an astonished Sybil. "All of it?"

"By Saint Elfleda, it is."

"And have you been searching for Thorston all these years?"

"Beyond all else, it's the book I seek."

"Is the book truly so valuable?"

"It contains all the evil magic of Northumbria. Whereas it can only be used in these Northumbrian precincts, its magic gives what is desired, even as the desire consumes the magician."

"Why do you want it, then?"

"Since such evil can never be entirely destroyed, it must be kept from those who might misuse it."

"Why are green eyes so important?"

"As I told you the old religion held it to be the color of life. And if one wishes to live forever—as Thorston does—the means can be found there, but only in these Northumbrian precincts."

"But I told you, Thorston is dead."

"Are you sure? He was determined to live forever."

"Is it so wrong to want to live?"

"Wrong for him to reclaim his life by taking yours."

"What do you mean?" cried Sybil.

Wilfrid sighed. "It's the stones. They will renew his life. To make them he had to take the very breath of *your* life. When he uses the stones, he will live, but you won't."

"But I told you, he's dead!" cried Sybil.

Wilfrid shook his head. "Beware the book's magic. No doubt he chose you because of your age. If you would keep him dead, and thereby save yourself, bring the book and the stones to me."

"Tell me how he uses those stones."

"I beg you, just bring the book and the stones to me." The monk stretched out his trembling hands toward Sybil, hands little more than sinew and bones. As Sybil looked at Wilfrid, his face appeared to be as much a skeleton as a living face—as if he too hovered between life and death. Gripped by sudden terror, she fled back to the house.

18

Sybil, unable to free herself of thoughts about what the ancient monk had said—"When he uses the stones, he will live, but you won't"—made a cabbage soup on the brazier and served it to the others. The people ate with wooden spoons. Odo dipped his beak into a bowl.

"Some say that spring will never come this year," said Damian as he slurped his food.

"Perhaps time has frozen," said Odo.

"My father," said Alfric, "used to say that time is like an oxcart wheel—that it has no end or beginning, but only rolls."

"But," added Damian with a laugh, "the cart it lugs has nothing but muck."

"You are a vulgar boy," said Odo.

"Better boy than bird," Damian retorted. "We haven't found anything, have we?" he said.

The stones, Sybil thought to herself, but she said nothing.

"We're not finished looking," said Odo. "But even," he went on, "if it does not seem like gold, I know Master's test for it."

"As long as it looks like gold," said Damian with a grin, "I don't care."

Odo nodded. "A sniff of gold makes all noses sneeze," he said.

It was Alfric who, in his small pensive voice, said, "Mistress, what shall we do when Master Bashcroft returns tomorrow?"

"God's mercy," said the girl, her attention brought

back to the others. "I forgot about him. I shall put my mind to it."

Alfric's question dampened the mood. For the rest of the meal, no one spoke. They finished eating.

"Forgive me," said Alfric with a yawn. "I've not slept indoors for so long, the closeness makes me sleepy."

"You can sleep where you like," said Sybil.

"I'll rest on the floor," said the boy, and he went off to a corner.

"As for me," said Damian, "since your master sleeps elsewhere, I'll take his bed." He went to it and lay down.

Odo sat where the skull used to be, on the pile of books.

Sybil retreated to her straw pallet in the back room. After pulling the thin blanket up to her chin, she stared up at the darkness. She thought of the monk's tale, that Master had stolen the Book Without Words from him. If it had been stolen, was it not proper to return it to its rightful owner? Besides, its empty pages were useless to them. But there were the stones, which seemed to be important. Finally—reluctantly—Sybil made herself consider the monk's warning: that when Thorston regained his life, she would lose hers. It made no sense: Master *was* dead; and she, after a fashion, lived.

More than that: with Thorston dead, she was free. True, the notion of being unattached to anyone made her uneasy. Even so, there was something pleasing about it. Except—what should she *do* with her life? Something, she told herself. I must do *something*.

The sound of soft scratches coming down the hall-way reached her ears. In a moment, Odo peered into her face.

"Sybil," said the raven, his voice a croaked whisper. "I wish to acknowledge I've spoken ill of you too often. I've been unkind. My only excuse is that a sharp master makes for a dull servant. Will you forgive me?"

"I'm trying."

"And will there be no secrets between us?" said the bird.

"I'm weary with secrets," said Sybil. "Let me sleep."

"As God is my witness," said Odo, "once I fly again, I'll leave you. You'll not be bothered by me again."

Sybil, wondering what would she do without Odo, felt pain. But afraid the bird would mock her if she confessed such soft thoughts, she said nothing.

"You have no heart," said Odo, and he hopped away.

As the raven pattered down the hallway, Sybil's thoughts concentrated on the stones. She wished the monk had told her how they were to be used. She also wished she had not fled so quickly from him. She hoped he would return.

As Sybil drifted off to sleep, she wondered if it had been wrong to tell Odo where she'd put the stones. I must trust him, she told herself. I must. He's my only friend.

"Unfeeling girl," Odo muttered as he retreated to the front room. "Why should I care or trust her?" He reached the top of the steps, paused, and looked toward the back room. Seeing and hearing nothing, he hopped softly down the steps. Upon reaching the ground-floor level he went to the closed trapdoor, stood before it, and extended one claw. "*Risan . . . risan,*" he whispered.

The heavy door trembled as it struggled to rise.

"*Risan . . . risan,*" the bird repeated, somewhat louder.

The door quivered anew, strained to open, but failed and settled back.

"My magic is too weak," moaned Odo. "I still need her." Softly, he returned to the room and went to his column of books and tried to sleep.

In the back room Sybil remained awake. Wishing she had said spoken more kindly to Odo, she got up and padded into the front room.

All was still: Damian lay asleep in Thorston's bed, breathing deeply. Alfric was curled up in a corner, eyes closed, his thumb in his mouth. Seeing that Odo had his head tucked under a wing—apparently asleep—she decided she'd wait until the morning to speak to him.

Instead she went to the window and pulled aside the leather curtain, hoping to see Brother Wilfrid. The courtyard was deserted. In the clear sky, an all but full moon cast pale light into the room. She turned. On the table lay the Book Without Words, its pages glowing in the moonlight. The monk had said it was evil. Perhaps, she thought, it would be better not to read it. And the stones . . .

She went to the foot of Thorston's bed, knelt, and opened the chest. A sweet, springlike smell wafted up. As she held the chest lid up with one hand, with the other, she moved aside the bolt of cloth under which she had hidden the stones. She gasped. The three stones were glowing. But even as Sybil gazed at them, she thought she heard the sound of someone stirring across the room. In haste, she covered the stones, lowered the lid, and crept back to her room.

On her pallet she kept thinking about the stones. That there was something magical about them, she had no doubt. The monk said they restored life. But how? She resolved to speak to the monk and ask him for an explanation.

21

In the front room, Alfric, his head full of worry, had not been able to sleep. The death and burial of Master Thorston made him think upon his parents and their death. It brought tears to his eyes.

He also thought about Sybil. He was touched by her sympathy. How long it had been since anyone had been kind to him! The last thing he wanted was to return to Bashcroft. The boy prayed she would let him stay with her.

Even as Alfric had the thought, he saw her enter the room and look about. Feigning sleep, he closed his eyes partway and watched her pull aside the leather curtain from the front window. When moonlight filled the room, he shut his eyes and waited until he heard her go back down the hallway.

Once she had gone, he propped himself up on an elbow and peered about. It occurred to him that Sybil might let him stay if he could do something she wanted, something that would make her desirous of keeping him. Something like—the reading of that book: if he could find a way to read it, she might look with favor upon him.

Seeing that Damian was asleep and snoring on the alchemist's bed, and that the raven had his head tucked under a wing, Alfric went to the table where the Book Without Words lay.

Illuminated by moonlight, its stiff, yellow parchment pages seemed to have their own glow. Gingerly, Alfric touched one sheet. The scraped parchment made his fingertips tingle. One by one, he turned over the leaves. Each page appeared the same—blank. Or did it?

Bending closer, he scrutinized them hard, wanting with all his desire to see *something*. As he concentrated, faint lines began to appear—lines he was sure had not been there before. They were indistinct squiggles—but they were there. He stared harder. The lines became clearer. They became *words*. Alfric's heart began to pound.

Alarmed, Alfric backed away. The chill air made him shiver. He must be careful. Without question there *was* magic here. But he didn't want to antagonize the girl. Perhaps he was doing something wrong. He went down the hallway toward her room.

"Mistress?" he called to Sybil. She opened her eyes.

"Are you awake?" Alfric whispered.

"Yes."

"I can't sleep. And I'm cold. May I stay close to you?"

"Of course."

The boy crept close to her. She was thin but warm. "May God bless you," he said in a choked voice. "You are the kindest lady in the world."

As Sybil drew the frail boy close, she realized something: Odo had apologized to her. The monk had said he needed her. The boy had blessed her. In all her life no one had ever said or done any of those things. Here, in one day, were all three. Was that not a kind of magic?

22

From his perch on the books, Odo had watched Alfric examine the Book Without Words, then move into the back room. As soon as the boy had gone, the raven fluttered over to the book and gazed at it. He saw nothing. Agitated, he hopped over to the chest at the foot of

Thorston's bed. After making sure no one was watching, he lifted a claw and said, "*Risan ... risan.*" When the chest lid opened, he hopped upon its edge and peered inside. The sweet smell rose up. He was just about to jump into the chest when he heard a loud *bang*. The sound came from the ground level. Alarmed, the raven leaped out of the chest and muttered some words. As soon as the chest lid lowered, Odo retreated to his roost. Head cocked, he sat and listened intently.

23

The same sound Odo heard woke Sybil from her shallow sleep. Disentangling herself from Alfric, she sat up. The noise seemed to have come from below, on the ground floor. She listened. Within moments there were new sounds: grunts and groans, the sounds of someone laboring.

Sybil jumped up and moved halfway down the hall to listen. The sounds resumed. Recalling that she had barred the front door, the only sense she could make of the sounds was that someone had broken in. Perhaps it was through the old stone wall. The stones, she knew, were none too firm.

She crept into the main room. Moonlight

streamed in, bringing radiance to the top of the steps. She heard more grunts and groans followed by the unmistakable sound of heavy breathing.

"Odo," she whispered across the room. "Someone's in the house."

The raven lifted his head. "I hear." He stood, head cocked, beak open—an attitude of intense listening.

"Do you think it's the reeve?" said Sybil. "Could he have come through that back way—through the old city walls?"

"It's blocked," said Odo.

A loud boom echoed from below, loud enough to make Sybil jump. What, she thought, if it's Brother Wilfrid coming for the book?

"Odo," said Sybil, "I didn't tell you, but I saw—"

"Quiet!" hissed the bird. "That's . . . the trapdoor."

Breathless, Sybil listened as more sounds came: the unmistakable sound of footsteps could be heard moving toward the room.

A form, lit up by the moonlight, rose up from the well of the steps. Head. Shoulders. Body. A human shape.

"Dear God . . ." whispered Sybil, holding her breath.

The person stepped into the circle of moonlight that lay upon the floor at the top of the stairwell. A face.

Sybil gasped. It was the face of the man they had just buried, Master Thorston.

24

Speechless with astonishment, Sybil stared at Thorston. That it was the master, she had not the slightest doubt. Yet there was something different about him, but nothing she could grasp.

Thorston stood at the top of the stairs, motionless. Traces of dirt clung to his hair, face, and beard. His tattered blue robe was smudged. His hands and fingers were encrusted with dirt. Slowly, he moved his head, scanning the room, although there was no hint he was aware of anyone's presence.

Thorston, paying no heed to Sybil and Odo, came forward slowly. Sybil backed to one side of the room. Odo retreated to his book column.

When he reached the brazier and the iron pot with its mixture—the one he had been working on—Thorston gazed at it, and then reached inside. Momentarily, he held his hand there—as if feeling for something—only to withdraw it, filthier than before— but empty. "The stones," he said in a loud, angry voice. "Where are they?"

Sybil was too frightened to answer.

Grimacing enough to reveal teeth, Thorston continued to survey the room, without suggesting he was aware of those watching. In the end he turned toward his bed. Whether he saw the sleeping Damian, Sybil could not tell. He simply walked to the bed and lay down by the boy's side. Damian stirred. "Blessed Saint Dunstan," he muttered. "If I cannot sleep in peace . . ." The boy sat up and looked for the cause of his discomfort. "This was to be my—" he began to protest, then halted.

Sybil held her breath.

"God the mighty!" Damian screamed and leaped out of the bed. "It's *him*!"

Sybil darted forward and clamped a hand over his mouth from behind. "Be still," she commanded.

Only when Damian ceased to struggle did Sybil take away her hand.

"Is that . . . your master?" asked Damian.

"Yes."

"Is he . . . dead . . . or alive?"

"I'm not certain," said Sybil. She stood by Damian's side, staring at Thorston. Odo fluttered up to her shoulder. A sleepy Alfric—woken by the commotion—crept from the back room to see what the matter was. When he saw Thorston, he took Sybil's hand in his. "Has your master . . . returned?" he asked.

"I think so," she replied. "Odo, go to him. See if he's . . . alive."

The raven hesitated before he fluttered his wings and landed on the bed. He hopped the length of the old man's arm. When he reached shoulder level, he cocked his head first one way and then another before jumping on the old man's chest.

Thorston stirred, but did not waken.

The raven drew closer to his face. "Master," he croaked, "are you . . . are you . . . living?"

"Go away, you filthy bird," muttered Thorston. "I need to sleep." With a sweep of his hand he brushed Odo away.

Sybil, Odo, Alfric, and Damian scurried to the far side of the room, where they huddled, eyes on Thorston.

"No doubt," said Odo, bobbing his head. "He's alive."

"Did you feel him?" Sybil asked Damian.

"He was trying to take over the bed. Which—may I remind you—was supposed to be mine."

"It *is* his bed," said Odo.

"If a person dies," said Damian, "he should stay dead and not reclaim his bed. It's rude."

Alfric tugged at Sybil's hand. "Mistress," he asked, "is that truly him? Or his spirit?"

"I'm not sure," she said. "Wait here." She tiptoed to the steps and stopped halfway to the ground floor. From that vantage point she could see that the trapdoor was open. Dirt from the grave had been thrown to one side. The grave was empty.

She rejoined the others. "He's come back from his grave," she announced.

"How could he do that?" asked Alfric.

"I don't know," said Sybil. But in her head she heard the monk's words: "He *will live, but you won't.*"

DAWN CAME to Fulworth, and with it, a drizzling rain. Lowering light hung heavy in the chilly air. When the bells of Saint Osyth's rang for prime, they pealed with glum solemnity.

Sybil, fascinated as much as she was fearful as to what Thorston might do, had kept watch all night. So had the two boys and Odo. But when the morning chimes rang, Damian, grumbling how tedious it was to observe a dead man at his slumbers, went off to the back room to sleep on Sybil's pallet of straw. Alfric joined him and dozed by his side. Odo, proclaiming exhaustion, returned to the book column and slept too, head tucked beneath a wing. Only Sybil remained awake.

Sitting with her back propped against a wall, holding her knees in her arms, she continued to gaze at her sleeping master. She was greatly troubled. When Thorston had died, she'd first felt a sense of abandonment. But then the notion of possible freedom had come, and with it, the chance of change. His return left her feeling trapped. Repeatedly, she recalled the monk's prophecy: if Thorston lived, she would die. How would it happen? Would he make an attempt on her life? Would it be by magic? What was the connection to the stones?

The cathedral bells pronounced Terce: midmorning. Yawning, Sybil walked across the room and stood by her master's bed. His chest rose and fell with a gentle, fixed rhythm. Now and again he grunted. She wondered if they had made a horrible mistake, if they had buried a living man. She reminded herself that he had truly died. She had witnessed it. So had Odo. So had the boys. They buried him to hide his death, not his life. It was Master who had come back. The return was his doing, not theirs.

But as Sybil considered him, she finally grasped what she'd only dimly recognized: Thorston had changed. There were fewer wrinkles on his face. His hair was fuller and darker than before. The beard thicker. His hands bore fewer blue veins and spots. Fingernails were no longer cracked, no longer yellow.

There were teeth. Thorston was some twenty years younger than before—little more than fifty.

While Sybil had no understanding of how it had happened, she recalled that the first thing Master had done when he returned was to look for the stones he'd made before his stroke came: the stones Brother Wilfrid had wanted.

She opened the chest at the foot of the bed. Pushing aside the bolt of cloth, she looked at the stones. Their sweet smell rose up to greet her. They were still glowing.

Shutting the lid softly, Sybil went to the front window, wiped her nose, and leaned upon her crossed arms. Rain spattered against the thick glass window and ran down in trickling rivulets. With a stubby fingertip, she rubbed away the vapor her breath made on the glass, and looked out. Despite the rain, the normally deserted courtyard was full of soldiers. Bashcroft was there too, giving orders. On the ground lay massive wooden beams. Sybil wondered what they were.

After a while, the reeve marched off with the soldiers, leaving the wood behind, the courtyard deserted. But as Sybil continued to study the beams, Brother Wilfrid stepped out of the lane and into the court. He stood by the well, head forward, shoulders sagged, hands clasped as if in prayer, sandaled feet in a shallow puddle—seemingly indifferent to the pelting rain—an image of patience and misery. Sybil sensed he was waiting for her.

She glanced over her shoulder. Thorston remained in his bed, asleep. The others slept too. Determined to ask the monk about the stones, Sybil crept down the steps, opened the door, and stepped into the rain.

2

As Sybil approached the monk, he lifted his ghastly face and looked at her with his deep-set, pale green eyes.

"Is he still dead?" he said, his voice distant, and to Sybil's ears, weaker than before.

"He's come back to life," said Sybil, pushing wet hair away from her face.

"Younger?"

"Yes."

"Which means he did make the stones and has swallowed at least the first of them."

"*Swallowed* them!"

"That is the way."

"Is it the stones that allow him to return?" asked Sybil.

"Each one he takes will make him younger," said

the monk. "They allow him to regain his life, his thoughts, his magic, and finally, time—in that order."

"Why does he do it?"

"*Why?*" cried Wilfrid, the wash of rain making it appear as if he were crying. "His sole aim is to live. Fearing death, his life is lived merely to stay alive. It will take a life—your life—to give him the life he desires."

"My life! How can that be!" cried Sybil.

"It's the stones."

"Tell me about them."

"Are they with you?" asked the monk, his voice rising in excitement.

"No. But I know where they are."

The monk sighed. "I must have them," he said. "But it is even more important that I have the book."

"What would you do with it if it was returned to you?" asked Sybil.

"I'd take it to where it belongs so it could not be read. As for Thorston, he can't survive without the stones and the book. Not only is the formula for making the stones found in its pages, the proper order is written there. There's other magic too. Only green eyes can read these things."

"Green eyes have tried—and failed."

"It takes great desire."

"What do you mean?"

"It's more than mere wanting. It's . . . desperation."

"Can't you take the book and stones for yourself?" asked Sybil.

"Look upon me," cried the monk. "He's strong and getting stronger. I'm weak and growing weaker. I need your help. You can right this great wrong."

"He's still my master," said Sybil.

"When he was your age he stole the book from me. He who steals, learns nothing. He who learns, need not steal. Save yourself; bring me the book and the stones."

"I . . . I don't know if I can," said Sybil, wet and shivering with cold. She took a step back, "What . . . if I don't get them for you?"

"Then he will live, and you will die. And I shall continue my life, which is a death without dying."

"Please, sir, is there gold-making in the book?"

"Only false gold," said Brother Wilfrid. He turned and walked away through the rain.

"If you can prove what you're saying is true," Sybil called after him. "I might help you."

"Then I will return," said the monk in a voice that faded as he disappeared down the lane.

A soaked and chilled Sybil ran back to the house and barred the door from the inside. As she leaned against the door to catch her breath, she tried to think about Thorston anew. But the only thing she could fasten on was what the monk had said: if Thorston lived, she would die. Wearily, she climbed the steps and went to Thorston's bedside.

He was awake.

3

It took a moment for Sybil to recover from her surprise. Once she had, she said, "Good morning, Master."

Thorston stared at her with his green eyes. "I'm hungry," he said. "Fetch me something to eat and drink."

"Yes, Master."

She returned in moments with bread and a flagon of wine. Thorston had not moved. "Master," she said, "here's the food you requested."

"Set it down," said Thorston. While Sybil retreated into a corner to watch, he ate ravenously until nothing remained.

Odo woke and stared at Thorston who, when he finished eating, went to his worktable. As he passed, Odo leaned toward him. "Master," he called, "I'm glad you are well."

"Why shouldn't I be well?" snapped Thorston.

"Do you remember who I am?"

"An old goat who thinks he is a raven."

Odo shook his head and ruffled his tail feathers.

For a while, Thorston studied the Book Without Words. Then he picked up an iron bottle, only to put it down and examine something else.

Odo fluttered to Sybil's shoulder. "He's no sweeter than he was—only younger," he whispered.

Damian and Alfric emerged from the back room, yawning and stretching. When they saw Thorston awake and moving about, they joined Sybil and Odo.

"By Saint Walburga, he *is* alive," mumbled Damian. "It was no bad dream."

"Was it magic that did it?" asked Alfric.

"I think so," said Sybil.

"Why don't you ask him?" said Damian.

Before the boy could reply, a knocking burst upon the lower door.

Alfric snatched at Sybil's hand. "It must be Bashcroft."

"God's mercy," Sybil whispered. "I forgot his promise to return."

As the knocking became more insistent, she looked to see if Thorston would respond. At first he did not. Only when the knocking continued did he shout, "There's someone at the door."

"It's most likely the reeve, sir," said Sybil.

"The reeve? Why is he coming here? What does he want?" When no one answered, Thorston flung down the tool he'd been examining and headed down the steps. Sybil, along with the others, rushed after him.

Thorston went to the door, lifted the crossbar, pulled it open a few inches, and peeked out through the crack. Bashcroft was there, standing in the rain.

"What do you want?" Thorston demanded.

"I am Ambrose Bashcroft, the city reeve of Fulworth. And you, I presume, are Master Thorston."

"Perhaps."

"It has been rumored that you are an alchemist."

"What business is it of yours?"

"Alchemy," proclaimed Bashcroft, "is both unnatural and illegal. Since you do not deny being a practitioner of that nefarious art, you are hereby commanded to provide me with your gold-making secret. If you do not, you'll suffer grave consequences. *Dura lex, sed lex.* The law is hard, but it is the law. And since I am the law, it therefore follows that I must be hard." He rapped his staff-of-office down like an exclamation point. "Have I made myself clear?"

"You have."

"Very well, then, what shall you do?"

Thorston remained still for a moment—considering. The next moment he banged the door shut and replaced the crossbar.

"Stop!" came the reeve's cry. "You're committing a

crime. Let me in." He pounded on the door. "The least you shall do is let me have my boy. Do you hear me! I shall hang you all!"

Thorston, ignoring the shouts, retreated up the steps. Sybil and the others followed. When he reached the top room, Thorston started toward his worktable, only to halt halfway. "Sybil!" he cried.

"Yes, Master."

"I'm plagued with danger. Where are the stones?"

"What is he talking about?" Damian asked Odo.

The raven did not answer.

"I must hurry!" cried Thorston, louder. "I told you to care for them. Fetch them."

"Yes, Master." Sybil went to the chest at the foot of the bed, knelt, opened it, pulled out the three green stones and held them out on the flat of her palm. Thorston took the largest and put it into his mouth, his Adam's apple bobbing as he swallowed. He stood there, as if waiting.

"But how can—" began Damian.

"Shhh!" commanded Sybil.

In a few moments, Thorston said, "I'm weary. Let no one disturb me." He went to his bed, lay down, composed himself with hands clasped over his chest, and shut his eyes.

After a few moments, Odo fluttered across the room and hopped onto the bed. He studied Thorston's face intently. Then he turned to the others and said, "He's dead—again."

4

"Are you certain?" said Sybil.

The bird jumped onto Thorston's chest and leaned close enough so that his beak all but touched Thorston's nose. "Not a breath," he announced. "He's as dead as . . . dead."

"It's not normal for a person to die *twice*," said Damian.

"Mistress," said Alfric, "you gave him something just before he died. What was it?"

Sybil sighed. "A stone."

"He ate a *stone*?" cried Damian. "No wonder he died."

"It doesn't seem to have changed him," said Odo.

"But there must be *some* difference between being alive or dead," said Damian.

Sybil shrugged. "In truth, my life has been a kind of death."

"And my parents," offered Alfric, "though they are dead, they still live in my thoughts."

"You're just playing with words," sneered Damian.

"Our lives," said Odo, "don't give us much else with which to play."

"I'd rather play with gold," said Damian.

Sybil went to the window, leaned on one arm, and looked out. Though the rain was still falling on the courtyard, soldiers had resumed working. She grasped now what they were building with the wooden beams: a gallows. Recalling the reeve's words, she had little doubt it was meant for them all. When he returned, he would ask to speak to Thorston. What were they to say? What if he discovered what had happened? All would be lost: the book, the stones—and them. She looked at the two stones that remained in her hand. She supposed she could just take them and the book and give them to the monk. But she needed to speak to Odo first, alone.

She turned around to face the others. "We must bury Master again."

"Why?" asked Alfric.

"To keep the reeve from knowing what has happened."

"Just don't tell him," suggested Damian.

"Damian, a gallows has been erected in the courtyard."

"It has?" cried the boy. He and Alfric rushed to the window and looked out.

"Why is it there?" asked Alfric.

"To take the reeve at his word," said Odo, "he means to hang Master Thorston."

"But he's already dead," said Damian.

As Sybil put the stones back in the chest she said, "You may be sure that if the reeve learns of Master's death, he'll hang us."

"*Us!*" cried Damian.

"I fear Sybil is right," said Odo. "Another burial is necessary."

"But let us pray that this time he doesn't fart," said Damian.

"Or fall down the ladder," added Alfric.

5

It was both easier and harder to bury Thorston the second time. There were no body noises, and the hefting was done with greater sureness. But Thorston, in becoming younger, had become heavier. Still, once they had carried the body to the basement, they were glad to discover that having previously dug the grave (and Thorston having dug himself out), they had a much easier time putting him back in.

"A used grave is less grave," suggested Odo.

"But still not gravy," said Damian, who had joined

in the work this time. "Perhaps the first time you didn't dig deep enough."

"My fear," said Sybil, "is that for Master, no grave is deep enough."

They shoveled the dirt back. When done, Alfric asked, "Please, Mistress, shall I repeat my words?"

"If you would be so good."

"Rest in peace," said Alfric.

"And be content to stay this time!" Damian shouted. "I don't want to do this again."

"Now," said Odo, "we must resume our search. And with the reeve sure to return soon, we'd best be fast and thorough."

The boys started to ascend the ladder. Sybil did not move. "I shall stay a moment longer," she said.

"Why?" demanded Damian.

"By Saint George, Master Damian, it's not for you to be always asking my whys and wherefores. I wish to speak to Odo. Be gone with you!"

Damian started to protest, but changed his mind when he took in Sybil's angry glare. He went up the ladder. Alfric went too.

Odo turned to Sybil. "What is it this time?" he said with a sigh.

6

"Odo," began Sybil, "it's those stones. You saw him swallow one. It is they that allow him to come back to life."

"How could that be?"

"I'm not sure, but the way to make and take them is to be found in the Book Without Words. And since Master swallowed another stone, he's bound to return." She considered the grave with discomfort.

"What makes you so certain?"

"A Brother Wilfrid has come to Fulworth. Years ago, Master—when my age—stole the book from him. Odo, the monk wants the book—and the stones—back."

"How do you know all this?"

"He told me these things when I spoke to him."

"Spoke to him! When? Where?"

"In the courtyard. Yesterday. And this morning."

"Where was I?"

"Asleep."

"Sybil," said Odo, "if what you say is true, and we give the book or the stones away, Master will surely not live again. If he dies, we'll never have the chance to learn his gold-making secret. We will have nothing."

"But the monk told me that if Master lives, I'll die."

"Why should that be?"

"It has to do with the making and swallowing of the stones. He said I'll live only if Master truly dies."

"And you believe all that?"

"You need to speak with him yourself. Odo, what good is gold if we're dead?" That said, Sybil hastened up the ladder, leaving Odo alone.

When the raven was quite sure Sybil was gone to the upper room, he hopped close to one of the locked chests. Rising a claw, he started to mutter, "*Ofan, Ofan—*"

"Odo," came Sybil's cry from the room. "Come here. Quickly."

"What is it?" Odo called up.

"It's Alfric," said Sybil. "He says he can read the book!"

7

"What has he read?" said an excited Odo when he hopped up to the second floor.

"It's about the stones," said Sybil.

As Odo fluttered close, and Damian hovered near, Sybil drew Alfric to the table where the Book Without Words lay open. "Tell us what you saw," she ordered him.

The boy brushed his red hair away from his eyes and stared hard. "It's . . . a list," he said.

"What kind?" Odo said.

Alfric moved his hand up and down the left side of the page. "Numbers are here," he began. "Top to bottom: one, two, three, and four."

"Is there anything about gold?" asked Odo.

"Shhh!" said Sybil.

"Not that I've seen yet," said Alfric. "But over here," he said, indicating the right-hand page, "there are words."

"Can you read them?" said Sybil.

Alfric nodded. "They also go from top to bottom. On the top it says, 'Life.' Then"—his hand moved down—"'Thoughts,' 'Magic,' and finally, 'Time.'"

"Four," said Sybil, who had been counting on her fingers.

"They're just words," scoffed Damian.

Odo, his tail twitching, studied the book intently. "It's the gold-making formula I want. Look some more."

Alfric stole a glance toward at Sybil. When she gave a tiny shake of her head, the boy turned some more pages. "I don't see anything about gold," he said after a while.

"There were four stones," Sybil said. "And four words. Odo, do we agree Master *made* those stones?"

"I suppose we must."

"And that he has already swallowed two. Remember," she said to Odo, "the time when he first died—or so we thought. He must have swallowed the first stone and come back to life then, too. Which is why I found only three."

"The first word *is* Life," said Odo.

"Just so," agreed Sybil. "Then four in all. Odo, recall what he said before his first death: he spoke about stones. That they contained life. Living again."

"Something like," agreed Odo.

"'Life stones,' he said. 'Immortality. Secrets.'"

"Then maybe—each stone," said Odo with a flap of his wings, "gives one of the things on the list."

"I must see those stones," said Damian. "Where are they?"

Sybil went to the chest, took them out, and put the two remaining on the book.

"Are you claiming," said Damian, "that each of the stones provided one of those things—Life, Thoughts, Magic, or Time?"

"I think so," said Sybil.

"Which ones did he take?"

"Please," said Alfric. "Perhaps they go from the first number to the last."

"If we think the first gave him life," said Sybil, "then the second must have been Thoughts. The third is Magic. The fourth, and smallest, is *Time*."

Damian reached out and picked up a stone. The moment he did, Odo leaped forward and pecked the boy's hand sharply. "Leave it alone!" he squawked.

"*Ow!*" cried Damian, dropping the stone. He sucked his hand where the raven had pecked. "I was only going to look. You need not attack me so!"

Sybil scooped up the stones and put them in her purse. To Alfric she said, "Thank you. You have been a great blessing. Come," she said to the raven. "We must decide what to do."

8

Ignoring Damian's angry looks, Sybil and Odo went halfway down the steps. When she sat, the raven perched on her knees and stared up at her, his black eyes intense.

"Odo," said Sybil, her voice low. "If all of this is true, it's we who shall decide if Master lives or dies."

"You mean, decide to . . . kill him or not?"

"I don't think we can kill a man who is already dead."

"Then—keep him from resuming life," said Odo. "I don't know but it's the same thing. Except it's not certain he'll return."

"Odo, he swallowed another stone."

"Perhaps he never really died."

"You know he did," said Sybil. "And the monk said if Master swallows all the stones, and thereby lives, I shall die."

"In other words, if we don't murder him—he will murder you."

"That's not fair. I say, let him die a natural death so I might live my natural life."

"What about the gold?" said Odo.

"Is that all you care about?"

"Sybil, nothing is more important."

"Why?"

"Only gold will buy the life we wish."

Sybil shook her head. "I'm young. Shouldn't I have a chance to live? I want to give both stones and book back to Brother Wilfrid."

"And I say," said Odo, "without gold, we might as well be dead."

"Talk to the monk," said Sybil. "Listen to him. You'll see he's right."

"If you insist," said the bird. "Just know that I'll demand some reason to do what he wants."

9

When Thorston slammed the door in Bashcroft's face, the thwarted reeve remained in the courtyard. It was the second time he had been treated rudely by those in the house. It made him angrier than ever. He did consider making a third try immediately and demanding—by force of law and arms—that Alfric be returned to him. But Bashcroft hesitated: there was something odd about Master Thorston, something unsettling. It made him cautious.

The reeve consoled himself with the fact that he had at least confronted the man—proof that he was real—surely not dying. What's more, the man had all but confessed to being an alchemist. As far as Bashcroft was concerned, even if he did not find the means of making gold, the least he should get was the gold already made.

He decided it was time to speak to Mistress Weebly again.

"As God is my witness," the apothecary said to him, "the girl told me her master was close to death."

"She lied. No man could be more alive. And I for

one am glad of it. I shall make this Master Thorston's gold my own, as well as his gold-making formula. My question to you, Mistress, is this: have you all the ingredients this recipe might require?"

"It was I who supplied him with all."

"Mistress, I offer you this proposition: once I have the secrets, I shall share them with you. Of course, I shall take most of what you make, but you shall have some."

"I'll do so," said the woman.

"Agreed. Then I shall bring my soldiers forward to lay siege to the house. The prospect of death is always frightening. Once I have the formula, I'll hang Master Thorston and his maid, take the house, and keep everything within. Now, Mistress, one final point: your apprentice is in that house."

"The rascal. I fear he overheard me when you were here. The very next morning—all on his own—he went off without a word. He has lost all favor with me."

"Then he too must be hanged," said the reeve. "On the morrow, I'll demand they all come out. If they don't, we'll enter by force of arms. My gallows is already erected before the house. But then, Mistress, *Dura lex, sed lex.* I intend to be as hard as death itself."

10

The night was cold and bright, the skies clear and calm, save for a few supple shreds of clouds shifting south. Moonlight streamed though the front window of the upper room, suffusing all with a pale yellow light. The thin barley soup Sybil made had been consumed. All was still.

Odo sat upon his column of books, preening his shabby feathers. Alfric had the Book Without Words in his lap and was studying it. Damian sat in a corner, fiddling with some of Thorston's apparatus. Sybil, leaning on her arms, gazed out the window at the gallows. She wondered if she were not like a condemned person in prison, awaiting execution.

Exactly when he appeared, Sybil was not certain, but she suddenly realized Brother Wilfrid was there. She had no doubt: he was waiting for her.

"Have you found out anything about gold?" Damian asked of Alfric.

Alfric looked up from the book, darted a glance at Sybil, and then said, "No."

"Then this is a fools' school," said Damian, tossing aside the tool he had been holding. "All this sitting about. We know what the stones can do. Which means we can have your master's magic by simply swallowing them. You can have the one for Time. I'll take Magic. What are we waiting for?"

"They are not ours for the swallowing," said Sybil.

"Surely they are no longer your master's," said Damian. "He's dead. Buried. Twice. That's enough for most men."

"You must be patient," said Sybil.

"Patient!" cried Damian. "If I stay another day in this place, I shall go daft. No, I'll stay until morning. No more. Then—I don't care what you say—I intend to leave. For now I prefer to sleep. It will pass the time quickly." He got up and lumbered back toward the back room.

Odo looked around. "Irritating boy," he muttered.

Alfric yawned and put the book on the table. "Please, Mistress, may I go to sleep too?"

"Of course," said Sybil.

Alfric brought the book to Sybil. As she took it, he whispered, "Follow me," and headed down the hall toward the back room. Sybil set the book on the table, glanced out the window, and then went down the hall.

Alfric was waiting for her halfway down the hall.

"What is it?" Sybil asked.

"In the book," Alfric whispered, "there *is* something about gold."

Sybil put a finger to her lips. "Don't speak of it yet."

"Why?"

"I don't wish to be tempted. Now, just go to sleep."

"Yes, Mistress." The boy looked up at Sybil, unexpectedly hugged her, and then went into the back room.

Sybil returned to the main room. "Odo," she said, "he's out there."

"Who?" said the bird. "Bashcroft?"

"The man from whom Master stole the book: Brother Wilfrid. I'm sure he's come to speak to me. You agreed you'd listen to him. Will you come with me?"

"And the boys?"

"They're sleeping. Master is buried. All is safe."

"I want to be sure they are sleeping," said Odo. He hopped to the back room. "They're fine," he said when he returned. "But I beg you, for safety's sake, don't take the stones. And promise me we'll go no farther than the courtyard."

"Agreed," said Sybil. "The stones can stay in the chest." She went toward the steps, holding her elbow out. Odo jumped upon it, and when he clawed his way to her shoulder, the two went down to the door.

Sybil lifted the crossbar from the door. As she began to put it down it slipped from her hand and fell with a bang.

"Clumsy girl," muttered Odo.

"Sorry," murmured Sybil. She pulled the door open and looked out. Moonlight cast a glow over the courtyard, bringing a silver sheen to the smallest of puddles. Overhead clouds drifted. The air was calm, if chilly. "Remember," repeated Odo. "Only for a short time."

Sybil nodded and the two stepped away from the house.

11

In the back room, a sleeping Damian heard the sound of the falling crossbeam. He sat up in alarm. Alfric did not stir.

"Girl!" called Damian. "Bird! What was that?" Getting no response, he went into the front room, only to find it deserted.

"Deceivers," the boy muttered. "I suppose they are at those chests below." He took up a candle and crept down the steps. He saw that the trapdoor was open, but when he peered below he saw no one. The chests remained closed, locked. Puzzled, Damian looked about and discovered the door's crossbeam on the ground. "Churls. They've gone somewhere without telling me."

Suddenly his face brightened. "The stones," he said aloud, and started back up the steps.

12

Sybil, with Odo on her shoulder, walked to the gallows, paused, and looked up. The noose dangled from the crossbeam like an open hand—as if ready to snatch her. It made her feel queasy.

Odo glanced up too. "We are surrounded by death," he said.

Sybil put her arms around herself to keep warm. But even as they stood there, Brother Wilfred, small, stooped, and limping, appeared. While an agitated Odo shifted about on her shoulder, Sybil acknowledged him with a nod.

"Ah," said the monk, his voice faint. "The raven, too."

"Do you object?" snapped Odo.

"A raven's feather is a necessary ingredient to the making of the stones," said Wilfrid. "Just as he took the girl's life by taking her breath, he took some of your being with your feather."

"I can spare a feather."

"Alas, bird," said Wilfred. "By so doing, he has taken far more than your feather. It is your life he's stolen, too."

Odo opened his beak but said nothing.

"Did you bring the stones?" Wilfrid asked Sybil.

Sybil shook her head. "We need some proof of what you say."

"*Proof*? That Thorston stole the Book Without Words from me?"

"You could be lying," said Odo.

Wilfrid stood motionless, as if lost in thought. The few strands of his hair on his head stirred in the calm air. His pale unblinking green eyes seemed to be gazing at nothing. "Very well," he said. Follow me." He turned and began to walk away.

"Wait," croaked Odo. "Where are you taking us?"

Wilfrid paused. "You asked for proof that I speak the truth. I intend to provide it."

Odo said, "How long will it take?"

"Not as long as I have been following Thorston."

"Sybil . . ." Odo warned.

"Go back to the house if you want," she said. "I'm going with him."

Odo remained.

Wilfrid, not looking back, walked up through the lane. Sybil came a few paces behind. Odo—now and again fluttering his wings—remained on her shoulder, hunched, black eyes glaring.

Though Sybil thought she knew the town well, she was soon confused as to where they were going. But though the monk said nothing, she plodded on, walking through the gloomy, constricted streets and alleys, over mud and stone, by heaps of dung and other filth. The only sound was what she made herself, feet squishing through mud. Occasionally Odo flapped his wings, but otherwise remained still.

The monk halted. "We are here," he said. They had come to the back of a church and were facing a neglected cemetery surrounded by a low wall of stacked slate. The graveyard was populated by crosses and stones, only a few of which stood erect.

"This is where Thorston should be," said the monk. "But your proof is in the church."

They went inside. It was deserted. A solitary light flickered in the old altar.

Brother Wilfrid went to the eastern wall and knelt before the large image that was there. Sybil, with Odo on her shoulder, stood behind him.

"Saint Elfleda," whispered the monk, his hands clasped. "I beg you; speak the truth about the Book Without Words."

In the stillness of the church, the only sound Sybil heard was her own heartbeat. But as she gazed at the image, the saint's eyes seemed to shift until they looked directly at her. Then the saint's arm, the one held in blessing, began to move. It reached out to her, palm up. "Bring the book back to me," Sybil heard a voice, soft, and as if from a great distance, say. "Its magic is evil. Since it cannot be destroyed, it must be hidden."

"What's so evil about it?" cried Odo.

"It gives what is desired, but the desire consumes the taker."

"My desire is to fix my wings," said Odo. "I need gold for that."

Saint Elfleda held up Saint Cuthbert's belt. "Bring me the book and I shall make thee what thou were."

That said, the saint's dark eyes shifted. The arm went back in its position of blessing. She became still again.

"Will you believe me now?" said Brother Wilfrid.

13

Sybil and Odo headed back to Clutterbuck Lane. At first they followed the monk, but at some point—Sybil was not sure when—he left them.

"We must give the monk the book and stones," she said, breaking her silence.

"And the gold-making secrets?" said the bird.

"Oh, Odo, wouldn't you rather live? Besides, the saint said she would fix you."

"Actually, she said she'd make me what I was."

"Isn't that what you want?"

"I don't like it," said Odo, "that all this living and dying is so mixed up. It should be one or the other."

"It doesn't seem to be," said the girl.

The raven remained still for a while. Then he said, "He didn't say we had to return *all* the stones. Perhaps if I took the Magic one, I could gain the secret of gold-making."

"That's what Damian said. Odo," said Sybil, "I want to live. And to do that we must return the book and stones."

Odo only shook his head. "And the gold?"

"Odo, there isn't any."

"The chests," said Odo.

"We have no keys."

"I still want to look," said Odo.

"When we return home," said Sybil, "I'm going to fetch the book and the stones and bring them to Brother Wilfrid."

"And then?"

"I don't know."

"You never cared about living before. What has changed?"

"I have learned something."

"What?"

"Master may wish to never die, but I have yet to live."

Within moments they entered the house. "You go up," said the bird. "I want to look at the chests again."

Sybil went up the steps.

14

As soon as she had gone, Odo hopped down the ladder. First he checked the grave and was relieved to find it undisturbed. Then he drew close to one of the chests, lifted a claw, and whispered, "*Meltan. Meltan.*" One of the locks shook, turned to water, flowed down to the ground, and disappeared.

Head cocked, Odo listened. Certain no one was coming, he lifted his claw a second time. "*Ofan, Ofan*," he murmured. With a creak the chest lid swung open. Fluttering his wings and leaping, Odo landed upon the chest's lip. He looked within. "*Ah!*" he croaked. He was about to hop into the chest when he heard Sybil cry from above: "Odo, come quickly! Damian has stolen the stones!"

15

Odo raced up to the second floor as fast as he could hop. When he arrived, a red-faced Damian was by the front window, right hand held aloft and clenched in a fist. A furious Sybil, iron bottle in hand, stood before him, not allowing him to move. Alfric, frightened, stood across the room.

"Give me those stones!" Sybil shouted at Damian. "Or by Saint Lull, I'll crown you with this, and then pry them from your dead fingers."

"They're magic," shouted the boy. "And since there's no gold, it's only what I deserve and need. I shall eat them myself." He opened his mouth wide.

With a raucous squawk and jump, Odo landed on Damian's head. As his talons sank into the boy's scalp, he began to peck around his neck.

"Off, you filthy bird!" the boy screamed.

"Release the stones!" cried Sybil, drawing closer with her bottle, arm cocked.

"I won't!" returned Damian. As he tried to swat Odo away with his free hand, Sybil dropped the bottle, darted forward, and grabbed the boy's arm, pinning it to his side. "Let them go," she shouted.

"No!" screamed Damian.

"Alfric," Sybil called. "Pry his hand open. I'll hold him."

Alfric approached timidly.

"I'll kick you," Damian warned.

Odo pecked Damian's head furiously.

"You're hurting me!" screamed the boy.

"Alfric," cried Sybil. "Do as I say."

Alfric darted forward and grabbed Damian's hand. Damian tried to kick him. Alfric responded by bending over and biting Damian's wrist.

"*Yow!*" cried Damian. His hand opened. The stones clattered to the floor. Alfric snatched them up and scurried off to a corner. As Odo leaped away, Sybil released the boy. Panting, she went to where Alfric stood, and held out her hand. He gave her the two stones.

"I'm bloody," cried Damian, holding out a red-stained hand. He dropped to the floor and began to sob. "I despise you all. You're low, filthy people—and you're a filthy bird."

"And you are an ill-mannered, thieving boy," a trembling Sybil called from across the room. "You should be ashamed of yourself."

"You all loathe me," Damian blubbered.

"What have you done to deserve otherwise?" said Sybil.

"You have all these secrets," Damian retorted. "But you tell me nothing. I'm sure by now Mistress Weebly will want none of me. I was a fool to come here. Now I have nothing."

"It was your choice to stay," Sybil said.

"You forced me!"

"Anyway," said Sybil, "you can't leave now. What's happened here must remain a secret."

"And we might find gold," offered Alfric.

"Stupid boy," yelled Damian. "THERE IS NO GOLD. We'll never find any. It's a cheat. A fraud. This Thorston is a disgusting old man who hasn't the common decency to stay dead. If I were dead I should stay dead. I hate being alive! I despise Fulworth. I've already run away, and now I'll go farther."

"Where will you go?" asked Alfric.

"What do you care? Do you think I'd take you? Not likely." He began to cry anew, big air-gulping sobs.

Sybil sighed. "Master Damian, we are all just trying to live. But we can't if we steal from one another, can we?" She sat on Thorston's bed and opened her hand. The two stones, one smaller than the other, lay glowing in her palm. "Do you wish to know the truth about these?"

Alfric drew near. Damian looked away as if he didn't care, but Sybil was sure he was listening.

"These stones," began Sybil, "were made by our

master a few days ago. They are his way of staying alive."

"He's bloody well failed, hasn't he?" said Damian, wiping away his tears. "And I'm glad of it. So why couldn't I have at least one stone?"

"Damian," said a weary Sybil, "we need to work together. And if we find anything of value, we'll surely share."

Exhausted, they sat in silence. Sybil gazed at the stones and wondered what would happen if she swallowed one. Would she become something else? Would she die? Then she remembered: she was going to bring them to Brother Wilfrid.

Even as she got up, Odo, from atop the books, bobbed his head a few times and said, "I wish to announce something."

They looked around.

The raven opened his beak, stuck out his black tongue, and then said: "I have found Master's gold."

There was stunned silence.

Sybil found voice to ask, "Is that truly so?"

The bird nodded.

"Where is it?" demanded Damian.

"Below. In those chests by his grave."

"They were locked," said Sybil. "Did you find the key?"

"I . . . had another way of opening it."

"Which was—?" said Sybil.

"It's what I told you. I can turn things—small things—into water. I did so with the lock. Sybil," he said in response to her accusatory look. "I told you I could do that. I did."

"Did you really find gold?" asked a wide-eyed Damian.

"You may look for yourself," said the bird.

Sybil shoved the two stones into her purse, grabbed a candle and, with the others, rushed down the steps and ladder into the dirt basement. Holding up the candle, she glanced at the grave. It was undisturbed. "He hasn't moved," she said, much relieved.

"God grant him a true death this time," said Alfric.

Damian was only interested in the chests. "Did you really turn the lock into water?" he asked Odo.

"Watch," said Odo. He lifted a claw to the second lock and said, "*Meltan. Meltan.*" The old iron lock shook on its hasp, quivered, turned to water, and dribbled into the ground.

"It *is* magic," Alfric whispered.

"Can you make the lock come back?" asked Sybil.

"I fear it will probably do so on its own," the bird admitted. "My magic isn't strong."

"Who cares whether it's strong or not," said Damian. "Open the chests."

Sybil and Alfric took hold of a chest lid and swung it open. The candlelight revealed a great heap of coins, most of them golden.

"Heaven's mercy!" gasped Sybil.

A giggling Damian pushed his arm up to his elbow into the coins. "A king's fortune!" he exclaimed.

Sybil picked up one of the golden coins and let it drop. It made a heavy plunking sound. She grinned.

"You wondered where he got his money," Odo said to Sybil. "Now you know: he *did* make it."

"And we'll share it, won't we?" said a laughing Damian.

"We can," said Sybil, her eyes fixed on the bright coins.

Alfric tugged on Sybil's sleeve. "Mistress . . ."

"What now?"

"When you dropped that coin it didn't . . . sound like gold."

"How would a beggar like you know anything about gold?" Damian demanded.

"There were times," said Alfric, "when my father did ledgers for merchants. I'd be with him often enough and he'd let me play with money. The sound of gold is not one I'd ever forget. There's nothing like it. But a gold coin—when it falls—doesn't sound like that one did."

"What are you suggesting?" cried Sybil.

"Forgive me," said Alfric, afraid to look up. "Perhaps they are false."

"Do you mean to say," roared Damian, "Master Thorston was no more than a falsifier of coins?"

Sybil felt ill. "I don't know," she said. "Perhaps because he made it, it has a different sound."

"I know the test for gold," said Odo. "I saw Master do it many times."

"God's heart," said Sybil. "Then we had best test them." She scooped up a handful of the coins and headed above.

17

As soon as they cleared a place on Thorston's worktable, Sybil put a coin in a clay dish.

"As best I can recall," said Odo, while the others gathered around, "we must make a solution of mercury and vinegar mixed with salt. It will turn green. But when you put a drop of it on a coin that is not true gold, the liquid turns blue."

"Do we have those ingredients?" said Damian.

Sybil looked to Odo.

"I'm sure we do," said the raven. "On the shelves."

A frantic search commenced. Since both Damian and Alfric could read, they took the lead, checking bottle after bottle, peering at labels and signs. It was not long before they found what they needed.

Following Odo's excited, squawked instructions, Sybil mixed up the concoction. Using a silver spoon, she scooped up a small quantity and let a few drops fall on one of the coins. Hardly daring to breathe, they watched as the green drop on the coin frothed, bubbled, and turned . . . blue.

"God's truth," sighed Sybil. "It's false."

"Try another," Damian urged.

Sybil tested two more gold coins. Four more. All of them. The results were always the same: *blue*.

"Then that whole chest is nothing but false gold!" said Odo. "As bogus as Master."

"According to my father," said Alfric, "the making and using of false gold is a hanging offense."

"So what," said Damian. "It looks like gold. Enough to fool people. If you don't want any, I'll be happy to take it."

Sybil felt a poke from Alfric. "What is it?" she asked the boy.

"Mistress," said Alfric, his voice trembling. "At the top of the steps. He's come back again. Your master."

They spun about. There, at the top of the steps stood an unsteady Thorston.

18

Thorston's hair was tousled, his eyes bleary. Though traces of dirt were about his robe and face, he appeared to be hardly more than thirty years of age—some twenty years younger than when he had last died. His skin was smooth, his beard and hair full and black, with not a trace of gray. His tattered and dirty robe was far too small for his erect, muscular body—as if he had grown a few inches. It was almost as if the man who stood before them was the son of the previous Thorston.

His appearance of momentary confusion gave way quickly to a fierce, hard look as he gazed about. "Why are you all staring at me?" he demanded.

"Master," said Sybil, "we were waiting for you."

"Waiting will do you no good," said Thorston. He moved toward the worktable. The boys—Odo was on Sybil's shoulder—stepped hastily aside to let him pass.

Midway to his worktable, Thorston halted. "Sybil!" he barked. "Who told you to clean the room?"

"You were . . . dead, Master," she replied. "I thought it wise."

"I was *not* dead," said Thorston, adding, "I was only pausing between stones."

"I thought something worse," said Sybil. "Forgive me."

"I forgive nothing," said Thorston. He noticed the small heap of coins on the table and picked one up. "Where do these come from?"

"Please, Master," said Sybil, "we found them."

"*Found* them? Where would you find these?"

No one replied.

"Answer!" shouted Thorston.

"If you wish to know—" began Damian.

Sybil put out her hands as if to protect the boy.

"I insist upon knowing," said Thorston.

"We took them from those chests in the cellar," said Damian.

"Who gave you permission?" roared Thorston.

"You were dead," said Damian.

"*Dead?*" Thorston echoed. "I will not be dead. I have no intention of dying. These are valuable coins."

"They're false," said an angry Damian. "Which makes you a cheat."

"Damian!" Sybil cried.

Thorston turned about. "Are you accusing me of a crime?" he said to the boy.

"Master," Odo called, leaning forward from the books. "I assure you, we know your strengths. We respect them."

"But unless you give me some real gold," said Damian, refusing to be held back, "I'll inform the authorities."

Thorston glared angrily at the boy. "Inform the—! What is your name and why are you here?"

"I am Damian Perbeck and I'm here because she"— he pointed at Sybil—"said you had gold. I was promised some. Will you provide it or not?"

"Of course not."

"Then I shall inform the authorities," said Damian. "Perhaps they will give me a reward when they hang you." He headed toward the stairs.

"Stop!" cried Thorston, pointing right at the boy. Damian came to an instant halt—as if held by iron hoops.

"Turn," Thorston commanded.

Damian turned, though the turning was not of his own doing. The look on his face was of great perplexity, as if he could not grasp what was happening.

"If your great desire is coins," cried Thorston "then *be* one." He made a flourish with his hand, and called, "*Cuneus!*"

The next instant—where Damian stood—where he had been—where he had been a person—was a heavy coin. For a moment it hung in the air, then clunked to the floor, spinning three times before flopping over.

"Master!" cried Sybil. "What have you done?" She ran to the coin and picked it up. It was the color of lead, and there was an image of Damian's face on it: hair clipped around his head like an inverted bowl, heavily lidded eyes, turned-up nose.

"I will *not* be threatened," said Thorston, turning back to his worktable. "Not that he was worth anything."

"But . . . Master. . . ." stammered Sybil.

Thorston glared at Sybil. "Was it you who brought these people here?"

"Master, you told us to fetch someone with green eyes."

"Green eyes!" cried Thorston. "All such must be avoided." He spun about and pointed at Alfric. "Does he have green eyes too?"

Alfric shrank into the corner.

"Master," cried a frightened Sybil, "I implore you—"

"I will not be endangered!" cried Thorston. "He must go too." He lifted his hand, only to be interrupted by a banging on the door.

Thorston turned from Alfric. "What is that?" he demanded, his hand dropping.

"It's someone at the front door," Odo said in haste.

Thorston went to the window and looked out. "There are soldiers milling in the courtyard," he said. "And a gallows. Why has it been erected? Why must I always be threatened by death? Indeed, why have any life at all if it must end? What have you done?" he shouted at Sybil. "And you," he said to Odo. "You, who I trusted. You're a fool. Well, it's time enough to be done with you, too."

"Please, Master," said Sybil, "the gallows is meant to threaten all of us."

"Why?" demanded Thorston.

"It's the city reeve, Master," said Odo. "He wants gold."

"What made him think there is any here?"

"We're . . . not sure," said Odo. "Perhaps it was Mistress Weebly, the apothecary. That boy—the one you just transformed. He was her apprentice."

The knocking on the door resumed, louder.

"I've no time to deal with anyone," said Thorston. "I have yet to finish with the stones."

"Do you wish me to do something, Master?" Sybil offered.

"If it will make the man go away, I'll give him some of these coins," said Thorston. "They'll turn to nothing soon enough." He scooped the coins up and went down the steps.

"Odo," said Sybil. "He mustn't."

"How am I to stop him?"

"Hateful man," she cried. "Run to the back room," she said to Alfric. "Hide. I'll tell him you're gone."

As Alfric ran off, she hurried down the steps—Odo

with her—stopping halfway down to look on. Thorston was at the door, lifting the crossbar.

"Master," Sybil called. "I beg you, don't give those coins away. It will only cause more difficulties."

Thorston turned. "Don't give me advice. These Fulworth people are fools. How long have I managed to hide from them? I assure you, they'll be satisfied with false gold." He yanked the door open.

It was Bashcroft. He held up a lantern and gazed at Thorston with puzzlement. "I am Ambrose Bashcroft," he announced. "Fulworth's city reeve. And you, from your age and likeness, I presume you . . . are the son of the alchemist, Master Thorston. Very well: I must see your father."

"I fear," said Thorston, "you cannot speak to him."

"Why? I spoke to him before."

"My father is dead."

"Dead," cried Bashcroft. "When?"

"Many years ago."

"But—I spoke to him today, right here."

"I assure you," said Thorston, "my father is no longer living."

A baffled Bashcroft stared at Thorston. "Are you truly your father's son?"

"May I suggest," said Thorston, "it's the rare man who is *not* his father's son. And you sir, why have you come?"

Bashcroft drew himself up to his full girth and

thumped his staff-of-office down. "There is gold within this house—made by your father. To make such gold is illegal. *Dura lex, sed lex.* The law is hard, but it is the law. Since I am the law, I must be hard. I have come to claim not just the gold but the method by which you make it."

"Then for your pains," said Thorston, "you are welcome to this." And he flung the handful of coins at the reeve.

Taken by surprise, Bashcroft bent over and hastily began to pluck up the coins. Once in hand he let his lantern shine on them. He was still examining them when Thorston slammed the door shut and barred it from within.

There was immediate banging on the door. "Wait! By order of the law. I must have all of your father's golden hoard. Otherwise you'll be arrested and hanged. All of you!"

19

Thorston went back up the steps, passing Sybil and Odo on his way to the upper room. When he reached it, he suddenly stopped and stood still, as if struggling to remember something.

Sybil came to the top of the steps. "Master, what is it?"

Thorston stretched and yawned. "I am tired."

"Master," said Sybil, "of late you have been often weary."

"It's the stones," said Thorston. He sat down on his bed. "They do that to one. But all the same," he said, "I think—" He turned his head one way, then another, as if looking for something. He opened the Book Without Words, studied it, then went to the chest and looked through it.

He swung about. "Where are they?" he said. "Must I rid myself of you, too?"

Sybil was too frightened to move.

"Give them to me!" he shouted.

Sybil held out her shaking hand. The remaining two green stones lay in her hand.

"Fool!" said Thorston as he snatched the largest, put it into his mouth, and swallowed it whole. For a moment he just sat there. Then he looked at Sybil. "Give me the last one."

"But, Master . . ."

"Give it. I don't trust you."

Sybil, knowing its importance, hesitated.

"Now!" shouted Thorston.

Sybil, flinching, held out her open palm where the remaining stone rested.

158

Thorston snatched it up and put it in his hip purse.

"Do not bother to bury me again. I shall return shortly. Safety is in reach."

Sybil and Odo waited in silence. After a few moments, Thorston yawned, lay back on his bed, clasped his hands over his chest, and closed his eyes. Gradually, his breathing ceased.

"Odo," said Sybil, "examine him."

The raven hopped onto the bed and scrutinized Thorston's face. "He's dead—again."

20

When Bashcroft looked at the gold Thorston had just given him, he was dazzled. All he could think was that he wanted more. But he understood he needed help to get it. What could it matter if the soldiers got some? As long as he got most. . . .

"Look here," Bashcroft called, with great excitement to the soldiers who had gathered around. "True gold." By the light of the reeve's lantern the coins glowed brightly.

"There's much more," said the reeve, "in the house. Enough to make us all rich. On the morrow, as soon as the cathedral bells ring for Terce, we shall lay siege to the building, enter, and take the gold. I herewith promise each one of you shall have at least one gold coin for your efforts.

"Remain on guard through the night so no one may escape from the house. By this time tomorrow," he said, "they shall all be hanged and we shall be wealthy men."

The cheering soldiers took up their positions around the house.

21

A trembling Sybil covered the newly dead Thorston with a blanket.

"I'm afraid I agree with Master," said a weary Odo from atop the books. "We need not bury him again. With Damian gone, I'm not sure we even could manage it. Anyway, I fear Master will be back all too soon."

"God protect us," said Sybil. She turned and held her hand out to Odo. The coin, the one with Damian's image, rested in her palm. "The boy was false in life," she whispered. "He's false in death. Is that how the book's magic works? That his desire for gold truly consumed him? How could Master have done such a thing?"

"I suspect," said Odo, "those stones he swallows not

only make him younger, but more powerful each time."

"Crueler, too," said Sybil. "And, Odo, according to the monk, when he takes this last one—Time—we shall have no more time: we'll die."

Odo fluttered to the window and peered out.

"Odo," said Sybil, "we need to bring the book and stone to the monk—now."

"It's too late," said Odo. "Look."

Sybil joined him at the window.

"There, you see," said Odo. "Bashcroft is showing the soldiers the gold. If I know anything about humans, that will make them hungry for more. Step out the door, and Bashcroft and the soldiers will only hang us."

"But if we stay," said Sybil, "we won't be any better off in Master's hands."

"I suppose one of us could swallow the stone," said Odo. "That might help."

"Odo," said Sybil, "whatever good might come of it, it's clear something bad will come too—perhaps worse."

Alfric emerged from the back room. "Please, mistress, is it safe?"

"For a while," Sybil replied. "Master is dead again."

"But—he'll return, won't he?"

"We think so," said Odo.

"What will he do then?" said the boy.

"We don't know," said Sybil. "Best return to the back room. I'll come comfort you."

The boy started off, then stopped and turned. "Mistress, what shall become of us?"

"I don't know that either," admitted Sybil.

CHAPTER FIVE

1

As the cathedral bells tolled midnight, the upper room was aglow with moonlight. Alfric lay asleep in the back room. Odo was crouched on the windowsill, bright eyes fixed on the gallows and the soldiers, who were either sleeping or standing on guard.

Sybil sat by herself in a corner of the room, eyes fixed on the bed where Thorston continued to lay dead. On the floor by her side lay the Damian coin—as she had come to think of it. Now and again she glanced at it: the image of the boy seemed to be glaring up at her—complaining about his plight.

"Perhaps," said the raven, "we could use

some of those coins Master made to pay ransom for our freedom."

Sybil looked up. "Do you think it would work?"

"It might," said Odo. "As long as they don't know the gold is false."

"I'm willing to try," said Sybil, putting the Damian coin in her own purse.

The two hurried down to the basement, where Sybil flung open one of the chests. She gasped. The coins were gone: each and every one had turned to sand.

"Blessed mercy," cried Odo. "Try the other chest!"

They were the same.

"My heart is breaking," whispered Odo.

The two returned to the upper room. "This is all my fault," said the bird.

"Why?"

"My thoughts were only about gold."

"You only desired to free yourself."

"I should have been content with what was."

"But you hated that life," said Sybil. "Besides, we may still have a chance. I suppose it depends now on Master." She went to Thorston's bedside and gazed at his unmoving body beneath the blanket. She wondered if the astonishing changes of age came slowly or suddenly. "Odo," she said, "do you think magic is nothing but life in haste?"

The bird shook his head. "More likely it's the other way around: life being the slowest magic."

"But magic all the same," said Sybil. She thought of the last and smallest stone. "Such a small stone," she said. "Time. Such a great gift. How odd it's the smallest."

"How young do you think he'll be when he returns?" Odo asked.

"The changes seem to work in jumps of twenty years or so," said Sybil.

"Then perhaps," said Odo, "he'll be as young as when he first stole the book from the monk."

"About my age," said Sybil. "I don't think I would enjoy his company." She held up the stone. "What do you think might happen if I swallowed it?"

"Perhaps you too could start anew."

"And relive this misery of my life? I'd rather not go far back, but start anew—from now."

She went to the window and stared out at the gallows and the soldiers. But she was thinking about what she had just said. "Odo," she said at last, "there is a back way—the old back entry."

The bird shook his head. "It's blocked."

"By the old city wall. You know how its mortar is crumbled in many places. It's that way here, too. Odo," she said, becoming excited. "I've seen you move small things with your magic. Couldn't you make the stones fall out so there would be a hole? If you could, we might escape that way and make our way into town—to

Wilfrid—without Bashcroft and his soldiers ever knowing."

The bird shook his head. "Sybil, I don't know if I can. I'm an old bird. My magic is borrowed and, at best, weak."

"Odo, to stay here is certain death."

"That's almost what I said to you the night Master first died."

"You were right."

"How would we find the monk?"

"Once we got out of here I'm sure we'd find a way."

"And Alfric?"

"He needs to come with us."

The raven bobbed his head a few times in thought. "All right. I'll try. Save for one thing."

"What?"

"Master has the stone."

Sybil took a deep breath. "Then we must take it from him."

"Thorston will be furious when he returns to life."

"Odo, if we wish to live we have no choice."

"What if in taking the stone we cause him to waken?"

"I pray he won't."

Odo ruffled his wings. "Then pray and do it," said the bird.

2

Sybil approached the bed, her heart pounding as she stared at Thorston's covered body. She darted a nervous glance at Odo, braced herself, then reached out and took hold of the blanket's edge with the tips of three fingers. Even so, she vacillated.

"What's the *matter?*" hissed Odo.

"To take from a dead man . . ."

"He would filch your life," Odo reminded her.

Sybil, nodding grimly, took another deep breath and slowly pulled back the blanket from Thorston's body. "Odo!" she cried.

"What?"

"He's much younger!"

"I don't care how old he is, get the stone!"

Sybil gazed at Thorston. He was a young man, smooth-faced; lanky and thick-haired, with full lips. Yet there was no apparent breathing.

"The stone!" chided Odo.

Sybil made herself look about his body. "I can't see his purse," she said.

"It must be on his other side."

Sybil began to lean over the body, only to pull back.

"What's the matter?"

"I'm frightened."

"You handled him before when he was dead."

"But what if he should come back now?"

"I'll help," said the raven. He fluttered across the room and landed on the bed at the far side of the body. With bright eyes he looked about. "The purse is right here," said Odo, pointing with his beak. "If you open it I can pluck out the stone."

Girding herself, and taking great care even as she held her breath, Sybil leaned over Thorston's body. She saw the purse immediately. It was tied to Thorston's belt. With her arm arched so as not to touch him, Sybil felt for it.

"Odo, he's knotted it closed!"

"Get back," said the raven, even as he hopped closer. With quick sharp pecks that alternated with pulls upon the drawstrings, he unraveled the knot.

"Untied!" he announced, drawing back.

Sybil leaned over the body again and slipped her fingers into the purse, and spread them wide so there was a gap. "Open," she said and drew her hand away.

Once more Odo hopped close, leaned in, then abruptly plunged his head into the purse. Next moment he emerged, the small green stone locked between the bills of his beak.

On the instant Sybil stepped away from the bed while Odo fluttered to the book pile.

"Perhaps I should swallow it," said Odo.

"Odo, if you do you will kill us both!" She held out her palm.

For a moment the bird did nothing.

"Odo!"

Odo leaned forward and let the stone drop into Sybil's open hand.

3

Sybil, making sure the stone was secure in her belt purse—where it clinked against the Damian coin—hurried down the steps to the ground floor, candle in hand. Odo rode her shoulder. Together they examined the old wall. It was easy enough to see the outline of the old entryway. And when Sybil poked at the mortar between the stones, it crumbled. "You see," she said. "It's not hard. I'm sure you can do it. Do you need my help?"

"I have to do it on my own," said Odo. He gazed fixedly at the wall with his black eyes and raised a claw: "*Feallan, feallan,*" he whispered.

A rock vibrated—and tumbled out of the wall.

Sybil clapped her hands. "There! You can do it."

169

"One stone at least," said Odo. He lifted his claw and repeated the words. When a second stone fell, he nodded with excitement and set to work in earnest. He chanted, and stones tumbled to the floor.

"It's exhausting," he panted, beak open. "Sybil, be warned, the magical things I do never last. At least I now understand why: it's the nature of the book's magic."

"But don't stop," said Sybil. "You're succeeding."

Odo went on until a rush of cold air announced he had breached the wall. Sybil peered into the hole. "Tumble a few more stones, and I'll just be able to squeeze through."

Odo continued. Sybil checked again. "There," she announced. "It's wide enough. Wait here and rest. I'll fetch the boy."

"Just hurry," urged Odo.

4

Sybil ran up the steps and into the back room. "Alfric, wake up."

The boy sat up with a start. "Mistress, is something the matter?"

"You need to come with me."

"Where?"

"I'll tell you as we go."

"Are we going somewhere?"

"Out of the house."

"What of Master Thorston?"

"He's still dead."

"Won't he come back soon?"

"Which is why we must hurry."

"And you'll not abandon me?"

"Take my hand," said Sybil.

They went into the main room where Thorston remained unmoving on his bed. Softly, Sybil picked up the Book Without Words and led the boy down the steps. Odo was waiting by the hole in the wall.

"Now," said Sybil, "I'll have the hardest time getting through, so I should go first. Alfric, once I'm on the other side, hand the book out to me. Then I'll help you get through. Odo, it will be easiest for you, so you'll be last.

The two murmured their agreement.

Sybil got down on her hands and knees, extended her arms into the hole, curled her fingers on the other edge, and pulled forward. It was a tight squeeze, and the stones scratched, but she got through, falling onto weedy ground on the far side.

"Alfric," Sybil called back through the hole. "Hurry now. The book."

The boy pushed the book into the hole. Sybil

grasped it and pulled it through. "Now you should have it easier than I," she called. "Reach for my hands and I'll help you." She leaned into the hole, found Alfric's small fingers, and gripped them. "Squirm and kick. I'll pull."

Within moments, Alfric was standing by Sybil's side. As he brushed himself free of mortar dust, she bent down to see where Odo was.

"God's mercy!" she cried.

"What's the matter?" said Alfric.

"The hole in the wall is gone."

5

Odo was just about to jump into the hole when the stones rose up and rammed themselves back where they had been.

Stunned, he stared at the wall for a few moments then lifted a claw. "*Feallan!*" he whispered. Nothing happened. He repeated the word. The result was the same. He tried pecking at the mortar, but it had become harder than before, and only hurt his beak. He told himself he was lucky he wasn't inside the wall when the stones reassembled: he would have been entombed.

Perhaps, he thought, if he rested, some of his magic would return.

Exhausted, Odo hopped away from the wall and fluttered up the steps and then atop the books. Shaking his head in agitation, he thought, She has the stone. What if she abandons me? She won't, he told himself, even as he recalled all the times he had insulted her. Be patient.

Greatly agitated, Odo tried to settle himself. Just as he began to drift off to sleep, he heard a sound. He opened his eyes.

Thorston was sitting up in his bed and looking around. "Where," he said, "is the girl?"

6

"But how," Alfric said to Sybil, "could the hole just disappear?" The two were standing outside the wall. It was cold, and in the sky the full moon seemed to be racing through new clouds.

"It's the book's magic," said Sybil. "It takes what it gives."

"We're not going to leave him, are we?" said Alfric.

"We have to," said Sybil. "We need to find Brother Wilfrid. Just pray Master Thorston doesn't come back to life too soon." She checked her purse to make sure the stone was there, tucked the Book Without Words under an arm, took Alfric's hand, and started off along the narrow path that ran along the outside of the old city wall.

After a while, Alfric said, "Mistress, who is Brother Wilfrid?"

She told him all she had learned regarding Thorston and Wilfrid. Alfric listened in astonishment.

"Mistress," he said when Sybil had done, "that time you made the skull rise; was that magic you had learned from the book?"

"Alfric, I can't read, so I took nothing from the book. That's why we needed you—and your green eyes."

"But you said you had magic."

"I said so only for Damian's sake. It was Odo who made the skull rise. And for his pains, it smashed."

"Did he read the book?"

"What magic he knew he learned by watching Thorston. As you saw, Odo's magic is not very strong."

"Mistress," said Alfric, "as I told you, the book has other magic. I did see it."

Sybil halted and looked at the boy.

"Is that . . . wrong to say?" Alfric asked beneath her steady gaze.

"Other than gold-making, what kind of magic did you see?"

"Shall I tell it to you now?"

"No," Sybil said after a moment. "It's better I don't know."

"Why?"

"The magic is false. It will turn against you. Now, enough chatter. We need to get back into town and then find the monk."

They continued silently along the path.

Suddenly Sybil stopped, set the Book Without Words on the ground, and opened it. The blank pages glowed. "Alfric," she said, "I do want you to try to read something," she said.

"Is it the gold-making secret?"

"I want you to fix your desire on finding Brother Wilfrid. Tell me if the book reveals how to find him."

"What does the monk look like?"

"He's not very tall—hardly bigger than me—and very old. He looks almost . . . like a living skeleton, as if he'd been caught between life and death."

"Mistress!" cried Alfric. "I know the man. He found me on the street. It was he who brought me to . . ." He faltered.

"Brought you where?" asked Sybil.

Tears welled in Alfric's eyes. "Mistress, I hadn't eaten in three days. He offered me bread if I'd let myself be given over to Master Bashcroft."

"The reeve!"

"The monk said in all likelihood the reeve would

bring me to Master Thorston's house. Which," the boy faltered, "is what he did."

"What . . . what did the monk want from you?"

"To . . . to find your book. That I might bring it to him. But, Mistress," Alfric cried when he saw the alarm in Sybil's face, "I won't betray you in any way. I won't." He threw himself at her, hugging her tightly. "You must believe me."

Sybil put an arm around the boy, but squeezed the stone in her purse. "I do believe you."

"And you'll let me stay with you?"

"I will."

"I was too frightened to tell you," sobbed the boy.

"Alfric," said Sybil. "You must know, when we meet Brother Wilfrid I intend to give the book to him. It belongs to him. But—has he any other claim on you?"

"None."

Sybil looked down at the boy. He seemed terribly frail. "I'll trust you. Now, can you read the book and determine where he is?"

"But won't it—as you said—hurt me?" said the boy.

He was gazing up at her. The moonlight illuminated his red hair, his pale, streaky face and his green eyes. And suddenly Sybil had the thought: His eyes shine magically. Is that what the monk spoke of—the great desire?

"Perhaps you're right," she whispered in awe. "Better we find our own way. But we must hurry."

7

Odo looked across the room at Thorston. He was as Sybil had seen him, but even younger, no more than thirteen. His hair was unruly, body slim and muscular. His green eyes were bright with anger.

"Didn't you hear me?" demanded Thorston. "Where is the girl?"

"She's . . . gone."

"Where?"

"I don't know," said the bird, determined to say as little as possible so as to give Sybil the time she needed to find Brother Wilfrid.

Thorston remained seated on his bed, trying to untangle his thoughts. "She had no right to go without my permission," he said at last, as much to himself as the bird. Agitated, he flexed his fingers so that his knuckles cracked. Then he sprang up and strode to the window and looked out. The night's dank fog had risen from the river. It was seeping over the courtyard, reducing the soldier's lamp light to hazy, yellow smears. The soldiers—more ghostlike than corporeal—were asleep or on guard about the gallows. The dangling noose hung limply in the thick air like a hunting snare.

Odo, watching his master, shifted uneasily on the book pile and fluttered his wings. He wondered when Thorston would notice that the Book Without Words—and the stone—were gone.

"There are more soldiers than before," said Thorston. "And the gallows seems to be in readiness."

"It's the town reeve, Master. Don't you recall? You gave him gold. No doubt it whet his appetite for more."

Thorston laughed. "It's only false gold—as he'll learn soon enough."

"Which means he'll become even more furious than he is," said Odo. "More determined to hang you."

"He won't find me."

"Are you going somewhere?"

"He'll be looking for someone who doesn't exist. I look very different now," said Thorston. "Hardly more than a boy. That girl's age." He grinned. "He won't notice me. Being a child is the best disguise."

The thought seemed to remind him: he walked to the back room, only to return. "That boy—the one with green eyes—he's gone. Did he go with the girl?"

"I . . . think so."

Thorston considered for a moment. "It doesn't

matter," he finally said. "She'll not survive for long. No more than you."

Uneasy, Odo shifted about. "Why?" he asked.

"When I fully regain my life with that final stone, you'll both lose yours."

"And all my loyalty to you," said Odo, "was it for naught?"

"Loyalty!" scoffed Thorston. "What has that to do with anything? Living is my life. Have you any idea how difficult it has been to preserve myself for this moment? To avoid accidents, illness, and violence. Think how hard it is to keep oneself from death!"

"To what purpose, Master?" said Odo.

"To begin my whole life again," said Thorston. "I've outwitted death."

"Ah, Master," said the bird with a shake of his head, "what good was that life, if, by avoiding death, you didn't live?"

"Don't preach to me," said a scowling Thorston. He ran back to the window and looked out. "How did the girl and the boy get away?" he demanded. "They couldn't have gotten past those soldiers."

The raven said nothing.

"Tell me," cried Thorston, turning and pointing right at Odo in the same fashion he had pointed at Damian. "Or I shall turn you—"

"The back entrance," cried Odo in alarm.

"The *walled* one?"

"Yes, Master."

"Not possible!"

"Look for yourself."

Thorston hurried down the steps and examined the wall. Finding it solid he ran back up and said, "You're lying. There's no hole there."

Stung, Odo said, "I learned some of your magic, Master. Enough to allow them to escape. I made a hole in the wall."

"Knave! But then, she doesn't matter," he said. "She's only a servant. A nothing. Anyway, she'll die soon, like you. But I've a good mind to first turn you back to what you once were."

Odo leaned forward. "What was I?"

Thorston shrugged. "What difference does it make?"

"Then why did you make me a raven?"

"Because black feathers are part of the formula for making the life stones—by which I'll live—and you'll die." Suddenly, Thorston halted. His hand went to his hip purse. He felt it. "The stone!" he cried. "Where is it?"

Odo, his head cocked, looked at Thorston.

"Did the girl take it?"

"I don't know."

Thorston moved toward the bird, only to stop and

wheel about. "And the Book Without Words! Did she take that too?"

"You just said she doesn't matter. But perhaps she's no longer a nothing."

"Where did she go?"

"And how could I know. I don't even know what I am."

Thorston jumped for him. With a frantic fluttering of his wings, Odo leaped and managed to get away from Thorston's grasp by landing on the worktable. Thorston pursued him, but the bird scrambled to the window, then back to the bed. Thorston tried to corner him. With a great leap, Odo tried to get past, only to be snatched out of the air by Thorston. The bird struggled frantically.

"If I don't have the Time stone," cried Thorston, his hands about Odo's neck, "I'll die. But you'll die now if you don't tell me where she went." He began to twist.

"She's. . . . taking them back to Brother Wilfrid," the raven croaked.

"*Brother Wilfrid!*" cried Thorston, so surprised, he released the bird.

"The one from whom you stole the book," said Odo, hopping frantically away.

"How can that be?" cried a dumbfounded Thorston.

"He's found you. And Sybil is taking him what's his."

"When did she go?"

"How would I know, Master?" said Odo, making sure he kept his distance. "I'm but a fool."

For a moment, Thorston stared at the bird. "I shall not die!" he shouted, and rushed down the steps. Odo followed. When Thorston came to the wall he made quick, twisting motions with his hands. The stones tumbled out, bringing back the hole.

Odo, looking on, croaked, "I'm glad she's giving those things to the monk."

Thorston turned to glare at the bird . . . and pointed at him.

"Master!" croaked the bird. "Don't!" But all the same, he fell dead.

Thorston, not even looking at the fallen bird, squirmed through the hole. Once beyond the house he looked first one way, then another, before running along the pathway in the same direction Sybil had taken.

8

"There," said Sybil to Alfric. "The town wall is broken down. We should be able to get back into town easily enough."

It was exactly what Sybil had hoped for: a section of the old city wall had fallen down, the stones crumbled outward in a heap. With the incline not very steep, it took only a little effort to clamber to the wall's jagged crown. A short jump brought them back into town.

They peered into the darkness. The night's thick, damp fog had moved in, making it hard to see. "Is Brother Wilfrid near?" asked Alfric.

"I'm not sure where he is," said Sybil, adjusting her grip on the Book Without Words. "Or we, for that matter. Stay close. We'll go on until I find something recognizable. Perhaps Brother Wilfrid will find us first."

As she led the way along the narrow, winding streets, the mist thickened, wrapping about them like damp cobwebs. Their footfalls were muffled. Buildings loomed on either side and, in the thick air, appeared ready to collapse on their heads. Occasionally smudges of light could be observed behind shuttered windows. From the city center, the cathedral bells pealed dismally, as if announcing death.

"Mistress," cried Alfric. "Look there!"

Sybil strained to see. A figure—garbed in pale white from head to foot—emerged from the fog. It floated just above the ground, undulating in the miasmic air.

"Is that the monk?" whispered Alfric.

"I don't believe so," Sybil replied, her voice equally soft.

"Who . . . is it then?"

"I think it's Saint Elfleda."

The glowing figure lifted an arm—as if beckoning.

"She wants us to follow," said Sybil.

They followed the white figure as it floated in and out of the mist. At times it seemed as if she were gone for good. Then they waited. She reappeared soon enough—always beckoning. Sybil and Alfric kept on. But abruptly the figure vanished.

Sybil squinted through the fog. A structure, more blur than bulk, loomed before them. "There's something," she said.

They drew closer.

"It's a church and cemetery," said Alfric.

Sybil stopped and gazed at the cemetery. She recognized it as the place where Brother Wilfrid had taken them. "I know where we are," she said.

Sybil searched for some sign of Wilfrid, but saw nothing. "We'll look for him in the church." Moving cautiously, she made her way forward. When they found the entryway they stepped inside.

Inside the church an altar light flickered, revealing only a deserted hall. "She's here," whispered Alfric, pointing to the image of Saint Elfleda on the wall. "But where's the monk? Is there anywhere else we can look?" asked Alfric.

After a moment Sybil said, "Yes."

"Where?"

"The cemetery." Sybil, feeling uneasy, said, "I think it best that you stay here."

"Why?"

"I'm only going to look. The book will be safer here with you."

"Will you be gone long?"

"No. Sit yourself near the altar."

Sybil placed the Book Without Words upon his knees. "Best not open it," she said.

"I won't."

Sybil started to go, only to look back at Alfric. The boy's face was full of misery. She reached into her purse and felt for the stone. "You must to do something for me," she said.

"Please, Mistress, anything."

"It's the stone," she said, drawing it from her purse. "Hold it and protect it. It will be safer with you, too."

"But . . . what might happen?"

"I don't know. But if something does . . ."

"Yes?"

"Get the stone to Odo," said Sybil. "If you can." She put it into his hand and folded his small fingers over it. "Hold it tightly," she said.

The boy squeezed his hand shut. "I promise," he said.

"I'll be back as soon as possible," said Sybil. She left
the church through the same door they had entered.

9

Once outside, Sybil headed around to the back of the
church. With care, she edged along the perimeter of
the low slate wall that bordered the cemetery. Finding
a gap, she passed on through, then stopped to gaze
upon the dismal scene. The old cemetery was rank
with decay, choked with wilted and twisted weeds.
Over it the fog rose and fell like a restless, inland sea, so
that the burial markers looked like the fingers of
drowning men and women. The only visible life was
clumps of lichens, which glowed and winked in the
dank and dismal air with a melancholy, phosphores-
cent hue—like dying embers.

Not knowing where else to go, she wandered
among the stones, now and again stumbling and tripping on the slippery graveyard mire. Once, she caught
sight of something gleaming—a wee bit of pallid,
broken bone.

When the fog lifted briefly, she saw a shape
distinct from stone. She gazed at it intently, gradually

realizing it was the shape of a man. *Brother Wilfrid*, she told herself. Wanting to feel relief, but unsure if she should, she edged forward. The fog shifted. She could see. It was Thorston.

10

Inside the church, Alfric sat motionless with the Book Without Words resting heavily on his knees. The church's emptiness unsettled him, making him almost afraid to breathe. It did not help that the large eyes of Saint Elfleda seemed to fix upon him. He squeezed his hands over the stone so tightly his fingers ached.

To ease the pain he relaxed his hands and let his fingers uncurl. The stone lay in his palm, glowing. A sweet, springlike smell suffused the air. Alfric's head teemed with images of bright flowers, fields of wheat, and leafy trees. He recollected something he had seen in the book: a magic for making food. Just to think of it made his mouth water; his stomach churned. He began to open the book, only to be held by a sound.

Someone had entered the church. The images in his head vanished. His hands clapped tightly over the stone and book. He strained to see into the darkness.

"Sybil?" Alfric called. "Is that . . . you?"

Alfric strained to see. Gradually, a figure emerged out of the darkness. It was Brother Wilfrid.

Alfric sprang to his feet.

11

The monk halted before him. His green-hued eyes seemed to glow. The strands of his pale hair stirred. "Do you have the book?" he asked.

"I won't betray her!" cried Alfric. "I won't!"

"I must have it," said Brother Wilfrid. "It's what you agreed to get for me." He sniffed. "You have the stone too, don't you?"

Alfric nodded dumbly.

Wilfrid extended his frail, clawlike hand. "Give me the book and the stone," he said.

"Please, I promised . . ."

"The book and the stone," Wilfrid repeated as he drew closer, his eyes fixed on Alfric's face.

Alfric tried to back up, only to be impeded by the altar. "Please," he cried, "she's been kind to me. She—"

"Listen to me, boy. When I have them," said the monk, "I will help her."

"Does . . . she need help?"

"She's in great danger. Now, give me what I asked for so I may go to her."

"I just want to help her," said Alfric. He was trembling, and sobbing softly, clutching the book to his chest, a tight fist clinging to the glowing stone. "Can I truly trust you?"

"Of course you can!" cried the monk, and he reached out until his thin fingers touched Alfric's hands with an icy coldness that made the boy gasp. In an instant, his grip on the stone loosened. It dropped, pinging on the stone floor.

Wilfrid bent over and snatched up the stone. Then he brought the stone to his mouth and swallowed it.

For a moment he stood unmoving until he reached out again, and this time gently pulled the book from Alfric.

Then the monk turned and began to walk away, taking the Book Without Words with him.

"Please!" Alfric cried through his sobs. "You promised to help her."

When the monk did not reply, Alfric smeared away his tears and hugged himself. A sensation that something was gone filled him. He looked around. The image of Saint Elfleda was no longer there.

12

In the cemetery a shocked Sybil shrank back from Thorston. He was very different from when she had seen him last: he had become a young man.

"Stupid girl!" he cried. "How dare you leave the house! You're my servant and nothing *but* my servant. Who gave you permission to come here?"

"No one," said Sybil.

"Look what I've done for you," Thorston went on. "An orphan girl, I gave you a home. I gave you food. Protected you. Is this the way you repay my kindness? Must I punish you?"

Sybil could not speak.

"But I will forgive you," said Thorston, his voice softening. "Just give me the book and the last stone."

Sybil backed up a step.

"Come now. Without the Time stone I have nothing. Do you have it?"

"No."

"Liar! Give it to me."

The measure of anxiety in his voice made Sybil look at him in a different way: what she saw was something she had not seen before in him—fear.

"Did you not hear me?" cried Thorston. "I must have the stone."

"Where is Odo?" she managed to ask.

"Dead," cried Thorston, his face suffused with rage. "Let it be a warning to you," he said, pointing at her. His hand shook. "Just give me the stone," he shouted. "I must continue to live."

"Why?" asked Sybil.

"Because I do not want to die!" Thorston screamed and took a step toward her.

"But why should I die for you?" Sybil said, backing up against a grave marker.

Thorston lunged. Sybil spun around, only to slip in the mud. The next moment, she felt Thorston's hand on her back, her neck. He held her tightly until, with a grunt, he flung her backward into the mire. She fell hard and turned just in time to see that Thorston had snatched up a rock and was holding it high, about to bring it down on her. With a sudden twist, she rolled away. The rock came down by her side, deep into the graveyard mud.

Desperate, Sybil reached up and clutched the nearest marker and tried to pull herself up. Thorston grabbed her, forced her around, and pressed cold hands around her neck. "The stone!" he screamed. "I must have the stone!"

It was then that Sybil, sure she was about to die, heard another voice: "And if I have it?"

13

Thorston gasped. His hands went slack. He spun around. "You!" he cried.

Sybil, struggling for breath, looked around, too.

It was Brother Wilfrid.

"I have the stone and the book," said the monk, his voice stronger than Sybil had heard it before.

"Then I'll take it from you as I did before," cried Thorston, and he flung himself at the monk. Wilfrid met Thorston with equal force, the two coming together with a crush of bodies.

Feet braced among the grave markers, arms encircled around each other, they tried to hold their places in the mud even as they shuddered with exertion. Thorston strained to his fullest, his youthful muscles bulging as he struggled to hold the monk in his grip. Wilfrid shook with his own great effort. They stood trembling, locked in one another's grasp, caught in the tension of mutual strength.

Sybil, watching, held her breath.

Thorston's grip began to weaken. His fingers lost

their hold. His legs sagged. "Time!" cried Thorston, "I must have Time!"

Abruptly, the monk threw his arms wide open. Thorston, no longer supported, fell. As he dropped, he tried to snatch at the monk to bring him down. With one blow, Wilfrid struck Thorston's hands away.

Thorston, on his hands and knees, turned to Sybil. The look upon his face was filled with dread and pain. He held out a shaking hand toward her. "I'm dying," he whimpered. "Pity me. I only wanted to live."

When a terrified Sybil made no move or reply, Thorston's begging hand dropped. He began to age, his body shrinking and shriveling rapidly. In a matter of moments he became old, older, older still, more ancient than he had ever been. His flesh loosened upon his bones. His muscles unhinged. His skin became a mottled blue and green and then turned to rot, collapsing. In moments, what had been a man became a mound of quivering flesh, fused into a foul lump of putrid muck, which quickly bled into the graveyard earth until not the slightest trace remained.

14

Weak and sore, Sybil picked herself up from the mud. She looked around. Brother Wilfrid was standing still, not looking at her, but at the place on the ground where Thorston had been.

"Is . . . is he gone?" she asked.

"He is. At last."

"How did you know to come here?" she asked.

"The boy."

"Is he all right?"

"He is."

Sybil saw the book beneath his arm. "Did he give you the book?"

"He did."

"And Odo?"

"The raven? I don't know."

"Do you have the stone?" asked Sybil.

"I took it," said Wilfrid. "I could not have resisted Thorston without. Time overwhelms all. Now I must return the book to where it belongs."

"Where is that?"

"Saint Elfleda will guide me."

"And then?"

"I shall have my rest." That said, Wilfrid turned about and made his way out of the cemetery. As the fog wrapped around him, Sybil was sure she saw a white-clad figure by his side: Saint Elfleda. Now it was she who carried the Book Without Words.

15

Sybil made her way into the church. Alfric was where she had left him, sitting before the altar. When he saw Sybil he jumped up. "Brother Wilfrid came," he cried.

"I know."

"The stone," he said. "He took it. He said he would help you. Did he?"

"Yes."

"Was I wrong to give it to him?"

"No, Alfric. Thorston is no more."

"What happened?"

She told him.

"What about Odo?"

"We need to go back and find out."

CHAPTER SIX

1

THE FIRST crowing of a cock could be heard as Sybil and Alfric made their way back to the old house on Clutterbuck Lane. They went the same way they had come, along the outside of the old city wall. When they reached the house, they found a hole.

"Do you think Odo made it?" said Alfric.

"I suspect it was Thorston," said Sybil.

They went through the hole, Alfric first, then Sybil. They went up to the room.

The raven was not there. Instead, there was only a scruffy goat, his short brown hair dirty, his horns crumpled, and his dangling beard rather thin. His brown eyes were full of woe.

Sybil and Alfric stared at him.

"It's me," said the goat. "Odo. I'm not certain, but I believe Thorston murdered me. But then I woke. Saint Elfleda was standing before me. She had done what she had promised me she'd do: transformed me back to what I used to be. But I'm not what I'd hoped to be. Look at me! I'm a goat! Now I shall never fly. What happened to the book? Perhaps there's magic in it to transform me back."

"Odo," said Sybil, "the monk took it away."

"And Master? The stone? What became of them?"

Sybil told him.

"Then I am what I am," Odo bleated.

Sybil put her arms around his neck. "I shall care for you."

Alfric looked out the window. "There are more and more soldiers," he announced. "Bashcroft is there, too. They look like they're getting ready to break in."

Sybil said, "We can get out through the back."

There was a pounding on the door.

"It's time to go," said Sybil.

Bashcroft allowed the soldiers to smash in the front door of the house. He strode forward, followed by a press of soldiers. They found the ground floor empty. The reeve banged his staff-of-office on the floor and bellowed, "I, Bashcroft, the city reeve, am here!"

There was no reply.

"The steps," he announced, and marched up. There was no one to be found. There was only Thorston's bed, the chest, which contained a few pennies, and the work space filled with the alchemist's apparatus.

The soldiers spread through the house. That is how they found the chests in the basement.

"Open them," cried Bashcroft. The locks were forced, the lids thrown back.

"*Dura lex, sed lex!*" cried Bashcroft. "The law is hard, but it is the law. And since I am the law, it therefore follows, I must be hard." He pushed his hands through the soft sand.

Sybil, Odo the goat, and the boy Alfric tramped along a dirt road some miles south of Fulworth. Though the wind was somewhat blustery, skies were blue, the sunlight clean and bright.

"Where do you think we should go?" bleated Odo.

"It was you who said the land called Italy is wonderful," said Sybil.

"Consider the expense!" said Odo.

Sybil touched fingers to her purse. "I have the Damian coin."

"So in the end, the poor boy shall provide for us," said Odo. "But how shall we ever find the place?"

"I may not know anything about Italy," said Alfric, "but I know how to get there."

"How could you?"

"Please, Mistress, remember you said it was what you wished. That moment, as we went along the wall, I looked in the book and saw the way."

Sybil smiled. "Then," she said, "as long as you don't use magic to get there, that's where we should head."

"Why no magic?" said Alfric.

"Because magic takes what it gives," said Sybil, "but life gives what we take."

"I agree," said Odo.

And they started off.

4

On a windswept and deserted island off the Northumbrian coast, Brother Wilfrid and Saint Elfleda stood in the midst of the ruins of the old monastery.

Brother Wilfrid had dug a deep hole in the sandy soil. He looked at Saint Elfleda. She nodded. Kneeling, the old monk placed the Book Without Words into the hole and covered it with earth.

For a moment, the two stared down, and then, side by side, they walked into the North Sea, where the roiling waves washed over them.

The Book Without Words remained where they left it—as unmarked as its pages.

FABLE: I have called this book a fable, a word that came into the English language in the fourteenth century. Deriving from the Latin word *fabula*, meaning a story, its English usage has come to suggest a supernatural tale in which animals speak and act like human beings. A fable is meant to exemplify a useful truth.

THE ANGLO-SAXON CHRONICLES: Brother Wilfrid's description of the events in the year of Thorston's birth is based on the entry for the year 973 in the Anglo-Saxon *Chronicles*. This extraordinary work, a compilation by many hands, provides the history of Britain from the start of the Christian era until 1154. It is believed to have been originally commissioned by King Alfred the Great.

ALCHEMY: The best way to describe alchemy is to think of it as early science, in particular the science of chemistry. Its practitioners sought a physical and spiritual understanding of the nature of existence. Much of their work focused on the making of gold and the finding of the "philosopher's stone," which would restore youth and prolong life. From a modern perspective, alchemy seems full of magic and superstition, but while there were no doubt charlatans in the field, there were many who were serious students of the natural world. While alchemy might have been viewed with suspicion and even fear, it would not have been illegal. Alchemists discovered alcohol, and nitric, sulfuric, and hydrochloric acids. The Book Without Words is sometimes referenced as a source of alchemic knowledge.

FULWORTH and NORTHUMBRIA: Though the town of Fulworth is imaginary, as is the monastery described in this story, the Kingdom of Northumbria did exist. Founded in the seventh century by Anglo-Saxons, it lies in modern-day northern Great Britain, between the Humber River to the south, and the Firth of Forth to the north. As a kingdom, it existed in one form or another until the tenth century.

SAINT ELFLEDA was a real person. Born in 714, she was the sister of King Osway of Northumbria. A nun, she eventually became abbess at Whitby convent and played an important role in church affairs.

For information about the saints referred to in the story, see www.catholic.org/saints/